Exclusive Bonus Feature at the End of This Book!

Read a Sneak Preview of a New Paranormal Novel,

"Wide Awake"

BLOODLUST

DANIELE LANZAROTTA

CREDITS

Written by Daniele Lanzarotta

Edited by Frank Monahan
Art Direction Meredith Hancock

Published by Rocket Science Productions

ISBN-13 978-0-9821823-8-3
ISBN-10 0-9821823-8-4

Library of Congress Control Number 2010934725

DEDICATIONS AND ACKNOWLEDGEMENTS

This book is dedicated to my husband, Richard, for his support and for his patience in relation to all of the vampire talk around the house and to my daughter, Briana, for being so proud that I'm an author and for looking forward until she is old enough to read my novels.

I want to thank my friend Christine, for her support and for being such a great test audience! As always, thank you Frank Monahan, Alexis Monahan, and Meredith Hancock for making this possible. I couldn't have asked for a better team!

Chapter 1

In and out of consciousness… That was how I assumed I had spent the last few hours. If only I knew what was going on… I had no clue where I was or what had happened.

I woke up in a white room. This time, I was awake long enough to call for help and within seconds, my parents were there with me.

"Hey honey. How are you feeling?" Dad asked in a concerned tone. Mom looked just as worried.

I had a terrible headache, but other than that and the fact that I felt lost and confused, I seemed to be physically fine. "I'm okay. I guess… Why am I in a hospital?"

"Do you not remember anything?" Mom asked, and then in a more calm tone she continued. "Just relax, Lexi. The doctor said that this might happen. You will regain your memory over the next couple of days," she smiled a forced smile.

I didn't remember what had happened. I wasn't sure to what extent my memory was compromised, but the last things I did remember were a call from my parents wishing me a happy birthday and a weird dream with Matt, my ex-boyfriend who had died in an accident that nearly destroyed my life. Even saying his name made my heart squeeze; it literally made my heart skip a beat…. I just remembered it being a weird dream with vampires who surely were unreal, although, it didn't feel that way. Whatever happened, I must have hit my head pretty hard.

I stared at my parents clearly confused.

"Someone found you and brought you in. All we really know is that you had a concussion…. But don't worry; all of the scans came back clear."

"How long was I out?" I asked startled. It must have been a while if they had time to run all of those tests.

"Almost a full day..." Dad said. "You do really need to rest, Lexi."

I would have argued with my parents and said that I was fine, but I knew that would have been a lost battle. So I nodded and said, "Before you go, where was I found?"

Dad sighed. "We really don't know, Lexi. The guy who brought you here left before he could be asked anything. The doctor said that you should remember what happened; you just need to relax and give it time."

Unfortunately, time didn't seem to be doing anything. A few days went by and I felt like there was a big black hole in my past and in my heart. It wasn't just the day that I got hurt that I didn't remember. I felt like I was missing bits and pieces of information from the past few months.

* * *

My parents and I had basically just gotten home from the hospital when I overheard them arguing. They must have thought that I was already in bed sleeping, because they were being pretty loud. It probably didn't help that my room was right above the living room where they were.

Dad sounded frustrated. "It is not time to tell her. She doesn't need the stress right now. Remember... the doctor said the less stress, the more likely she will be able to remember things."

Mom sounding practical as always said, "I know, but we need to talk to her. I know that we now have options, but she needs to decide...and we are running out of time."

What is going on?

I walked downstairs making plenty of noise so that mom and dad would be aware that I was coming; they instantly got quiet.

"What is going on? What choice do I need to make?"

Dad took a deep breath. "Sit down, Lexi."

Great! Usually, being asked to sit down was a really bad sign.

We all sat down. Dad took another deep breath. "Lexi, your mom's boss is transferring her back to Florida. We have to leave in a day or two."

"Well, I'm not going." I sounded calm, but the words just came out so fast. The weird thing was that I didn't even know why I said it. I didn't remember having any ties to anything or anyone here, but somehow, I just knew that I needed to stay.

Mom now met my gaze, "This is where your choice comes in, honey. You are eighteen now, so it is only fair that we make it your choice. Besides, the doctor insisted that moving you back is a bad idea. So many changes will only have a negative impact on your recovery…"

"Well?" I asked impatiently, eager to find out what my parents were up to.

"We decided to talk to a few people including your school principal, and there are three of your classmates who are emancipated and looking for an extra roommate… And even though we didn't like the idea that two of them are guys, we trust you. Besides, your school principal spoke very highly of them."

I didn't even have to think about it. "Sounds good. That is what I want to do."

Mom sounded relieved, but dad was clearly still worried.

"Great!" Mom said cheerfully. "We will take you by their house tomorrow. You are going to love it!"

“Wow! You have already been to the house?” I asked surprised.

“Of course! We had to check it out before it even became an option. You may be eighteen, but you are still in high school…. Anyway, they inherited the house from a relative. They wouldn’t even let us pay for rent. They said that they would be happy if you just handled your groceries.”

That sounded like a good deal. “Cool… Not that I will remember who they are, but, what are their names?”

Mom paused. She always had a terrible time remembering names. Dad finally answered.

“Anne, Lars, and Nicholas.”

Chapter 2

My parents weren't kidding when they said that the house was awesome. Funny thing was that no one would ever be able to tell that there were seventeen and eighteen-year olds living in that house by themselves. The furniture consisted mostly of antiques, old paintings, and other art pieces. They were all clearly family things that had been passed down from generations. The house was just so clean! Even my parents' house was never that clean… especially the kitchen, which in this house looked like it had never been used.

Nicholas was giving us a tour of the house. It was the second tour for my parents. "You are going to need some dishes for the kitchen and whatever else you may need to cook," Nicholas said as he looked at my parents, smiled, and continued talking as if trying to explain himself. "We eat out a lot."

As anticipated, I didn't remember Nicholas. My other roommates, Anne and Lars, were out of town, but I was sure I wouldn't remember them either. There were moments when I felt a connection as if I knew Nicholas, but it wasn't a good feeling: a feeling which I ignored. Nicholas was so polite and just overall… nice. Not to mention, it was adorable when he assured Mom and Dad that he would ensure my safety. When dad mentioned leaving me his car so that I could get around town, Nicholas told him that his car belonged to everyone in the house, and that it was not necessary for Dad to go through the trouble of leaving his car.

Don't I have a car? This memory thing really sucked.

* * *

My parents left very confident that I was in good hands. So confident that the following day they decided to go-ahead and head back down to my hometown, Pensacola, Florida.

Over the weekend, Nicholas helped me move in the rest of my things, and it was sort of cute how he wouldn't even let me carry anything inside.

Every once in a while, I still had a weird feeling about him, but for the most part it felt good to have someone like him around. The best part was that our interaction seemed to be pure friendship; even though he was hot, there was no romantic attraction which made me feel a lot more comfortable.

After getting all of my things in the house, we decided to just spend what was left of the weekend relaxing instead of unpacking. Nicholas promised to help me with the unpacking later in the week before Anne and Lars returned, and so we spent the rest of the weekend watching TV, playing Wii, and just hanging out.

* * *

Nicholas wasn't kidding around when he promised my parents that he would watch over me. That first day back to school, he managed to keep everyone away from me. He said that they would stress me out by trying to make me remember things that my brain was probably not ready to remember yet. Whatever that meant.

Somehow, we had all of the same classes. It was weird how some of the teachers were welcoming Nicholas into class for the first time in the semester, as if he had changed class schedules right in the middle of the semester. It was becoming a little annoying. When I finally had the chance to ask him about it, he said that his other classes were too easy, and the school principal suggested the changes. I thought that was weird, but I just let it go.

Finally, our last class of the day: Chemistry Lab. There was this girl in the back of the class who kept staring at me in a way that made my stomach clench.

"Who is that?" I asked Nicholas who was also my lab partner.

He looked back and winked at her before meeting my gaze. "That is Katie."

"Okay, what is her problem?"

Nicholas shrugged. "She can just be a bitch sometimes. Just ignore her and stay away. You definitely don't need that kind of stress."

I nodded and started to follow the instructions for today's lab.

Except for Katie's cold stares and Nicholas' over-protectiveness, the rest of the class went by smoothly. Actually, the entire day did.

Nighttime was a whole different story. Nicholas had a couple of… okay several girls either call the house or come over. The ones who came over didn't stay long, and he always made sure one left before the other one got there. So that was his flaw. He was a total player!

Finally, all four girls came and left. We caught a break, which was nice. I really did not like the way that those girls were looking at me.

I noticed that Nicholas didn't look as pale as he usually did, and he was not as cold either. He was one of those people who didn't like anyone touching him. Sometimes it accidently happened like when he took the Wii remote from me, or when I jokingly punched his arm after he beat me in a game. Talk about being cold-natured!

Nicholas' behavior actually made me really miss Matt. Our time together had been brutally interrupted by that accident, but I felt grateful that Matt had always been so faithful to me. Thinking about him was the first time I felt as if something in this house was off.

"You okay, kiddo?"

"Yeah, I'm good. But drop the 'kiddo'."

Nicholas smiled.

"Is it always this busy here?" I asked. "You know...with the girls coming in and out?"

He shrugged. "Oh that... nah, I guess I'm just having a good day."

There was an awkward silence, than Nicholas suggested that we unpacked some boxes. Lars and Anne would be back in two days, and we still had boxes all over the place.

We actually got a lot done that night. The smaller boxes were almost all unpacked. "I can finish these last few boxes," I told Nicholas.

"No biggie. I like hanging with my new favorite roomie," he smiled and winked which made my stomach clench. Something was definitely not right, but I just let it go and rolled my eyes at him.

I went back to unpacking. I opened one of the smaller boxes and found a black velvet box near the top of it.

I stared at it confused and then opened it to find a gold necklace with a small angel charm, and I froze.

Tyler!

That had been the necklace that Tyler's mom gave me when I went to visit her as a favor to Tyler. Tyler had been my boyfriend, my vampire boyfriend, who apparently had left me once again.

… And just like that, I became overwhelmed by the memories rushing back to me. I remembered Anne, Lars and Nicholas, standing in my driveway as I left after finding out that my high school boyfriend, Matt, was still alive and that he was now a vampire. Anne with wings very similar to the angel charm that I now held in a tight grip. And the last memory was the one of Matt at the beach about to turn me into one of them when Loren, Tyler's maker, stopped him.

Matt is still out there.

I sat there, my entire body trembling. I could feel Nicholas' gaze on me, and I could tell by his tone that he was well aware of what had just happened: I had regained my memory.

"What is wrong, love? Everything okay?"

I broke from my trance-like state, and I could feel the fury overtaking me. I glared at Nicholas who was displaying a sarcastic smirk, and I let it all out.

"You…you…freaking bloodsucker!"

Chapter 3

I managed to get Nicholas out of my room without any trouble, but it was frustrating that he was smiling as he walked out.

So there I was, wondering how I ended up in the situation that I was in. I was almost completely sure that Tyler was the one who tampered with my memory. His actions were the reason I had forgotten so many things, and that truly hurt. That had been one of the things he said he would never do to me. Another hurtful thing had been the fact that once again, he left. I was given two broken promises in one hit.

At that point, I was already lying on my bed crying as so many other things started to rush through my mind. There was Matt who was still alive, well not literally alive, but still out there. I was suddenly overcome by fear of what could have happened to him after he tried to turn me into a vampire that night at the beach. That had been the last thing that I remembered from before that incident.

And then I realized that at least right at that moment, I had worse things to worry about. I mean…Nicholas seemed like a nice guy now, but before, Lars, Anne, and Nicholas all seemed like bad news. What bothered me the most was that Tyler and Adrianne were just gone, which left me in a house with not just one, but three vampires who were probably just saving me for some sort of a special meal.

I shivered when I realized I couldn't do the one thing I was thinking about doing. I wouldn't be able to just leave. I knew too much, and they knew my parents. They would just go after me; they would go after my parents. I just knew that I was trapped.

All I did was lie there and cry because let's face it; there was nothing else I could do.

Just minutes later there was a soft knock on the door. I knew it could only be Nicholas. Still sobbing, I managed to tell him to go away.

"Not going to happen, Lexi. Don't worry, I'm not going to hurt you, but you either come out of that room, or I'm coming in."

I didn't say anything, and true to his word, Nicholas came in. Nicholas seemed surprised to see that I was sitting there in the corner of the bed against the wall. I doubted I could trust him, and I was sure I looked terrified. Not to mention, my face was probably all red from crying so much.

I remembered Adrianne telling me never to show any signs of weakness around a vampire; it would make my blood seem even more appealing, but something in Nicholas' eyes didn't show that desire. He looked as if he understood. He looked like he cared. This was odd considering that he was a total jerk.

Nicholas cleared his throat. "I'm not good with this human stuff anymore, but the crying has got to stop." He attempted a sweet smile which did not look right on him. "Is there anything I can do for you?"

I shrugged.

"Girls, ugh!" He rolled his eyes. "Alright, I guess I watch enough TV to know that girls go straight to ice cream when they are acting all… you know… like you are acting right now. Although, I have no understanding of how ice cream can help in any way, but whatever. Just be downstairs in five minutes, or I will drag you down there myself."

I started to nod, but he had already left my room. I knew he wasn't kidding around, so I did as he said.

I went downstairs to find him sitting on the couch. On the accent table by the recliner there was a bowl with Cookies-and-Cream ice cream.

"Sit," he said.

I did and grabbed the ice cream bowl. "Um... thanks."

"No need to thank me. That thing looks disgusting!"

He actually made me laugh. I couldn't believe that I was actually bonding with Nicholas of all people. Well, if he could be classified as a person.

He met my gaze. "Listen, we have to live together, so we might as well make the best out of it."

"True, but can I ask you something?"

He shrugged. "Sure."

I knew there was some kind of vampire law or rule that humans could never know about them; they saw human knowledge as a threat.

"I know what you are. I'm sure you are aware of that."

He nodded.

"So, why am I still alive?"

"Well, that is obviously one of the reasons why you are living here and not somewhere else...this way we can keep an eye on you. It is not like that Tyler guy knew what he was doing. We figured that you would regain your memory eventually." The reminder and confirmation of what Tyler had done brought tears to my eyes. I just wiped the tears on the sleeve of my sweatshirt. Nicholas pretended he did not see that and continued. "So, to answer the question as to why you are alive brings us to the house rules."

I looked at him confused.

"Anne wants you to remain alive and to remain human."

I knew that I was pushing my luck, but I asked him anyway. "Why? What does it matter to her?"

"I'm not discussing that with you. I stay out of Anne's affairs, and she stays out of mine."

Something about his eyes seemed darker as he said that. It made me feel uncomfortable, and I changed the subject to the first thing that came to mind which didn't seem to be that much better of a subject, at least not to Nicholas.

"Do you know where Tyler and Matt are?"

Nicholas now seemed annoyed, but yet calmer than when we talked about Anne. " I really don't know. Matt will likely come looking for you when he is ready and when he can get away from Scarlett. That is all I know."

Scarlett was Matt's maker from what I had heard, and just the sound of her name made me feel sick. "And Tyler?"

"Who knows?! From what I heard, Loren has been ordering him around a lot more than he used to. Anne said that they left soon after Loren dropped you off at that hospital. Although, I wouldn't be surprised if they return when they realize that you are still here…if they even realize it."

I nodded simply to show understanding. I hoped that he was right about me seeing Matt and Tyler again…

"You should rest now, but before you go, there is one more house rule. This is an easy one though. From now on, you can think of me as your own private bodyguard. I go where you go."

I rolled my eyes. "Like you weren't doing that already! Come on, I know that you switched all of your classes to keep an eye on me. You know… that is gonna get old quick!"

He didn't show any concern. "Do as you please. I can't help you if you won't allow me to help you," he said.

"Why would I need help from you? It is more like I need protection from you!"

He laughed and shook his head. "You have no idea how wrong you are, Sarah. You need protection from others."

I looked at him, startled. "Who is Sarah?"

Nicholas froze in place. "That is not of your concern." He didn't sound mad. He actually sounded sad, and that was all he said before he walked out.

Chapter 4

Right after Nicholas left, I realized that I was home by myself for the first time since I moved in. I wasn't sure how long he would be gone for, but I took the opportunity to go snooping around hoping to maybe find out anything about Nicholas, Lars or Anne.

I went upstairs where all of the bedrooms were located. Lars and Anne's rooms were across from each other. I hesitated before opening Lars' bedroom door. I had no idea what to expect, and let's face it, sometimes it is just better not knowing… but I was too curious. I tried to turn the doorknob, but the door was locked… same thing with Anne's bedroom door. I then walked towards Nicholas' bedroom door, which was across from my room. Just when I reached for the doorknob, I felt a shadow behind me and it felt as if the temperature had dropped drastically. I was freezing.

"Looking for something?" Nicholas asked.

I tried not to look too guilty. "Hmm… I was just wondering if you were back home."

He knew I was lying, but he just laughed. "Heard of knocking?"

Looking totally uncomfortable, I apologized. "Um… Sorry."

He sounded calm and relaxed. "Will you stop snooping around if I tell you who Sarah was?"

"I wasn't…" He smiled. Hell, he clearly knew I was lying. "Yeah, I guess."

I followed Nicholas downstairs where we sat in the living room. He turned off the TV which I had left on. He met my gaze, and with no emotion whatsoever said, "Sarah was someone who I should have protected, but didn't. After my mother died, my father remarried. His new wife was also a widower, and Sarah was her daughter. Once I was turned, things just started to happen to all of them. I couldn't exactly go around the house; they would have known what I was... but I was still around town... First, I heard of Sarah's mother disappearing. Then, Father started drinking, and eventually he went missing. That was when I went back and took Sarah with me... Not everyone was pleased with that decision mostly because Sarah was only nine years old, and they were all so sure that I would not be able to keep myself from turning her. Most vampires are against turning children into what we are; it is related to how pure and how much humanity a child has. It weakens even the strongest vampires. Then, one night while I went hunting, there was a fire and I couldn't get to Sarah in time."

"I'm sorry." I didn't know what else to say. "But why did you call me Sarah?"

He shrugged. "Sarah was as naïve as you. That is all."

For some reason I felt that if I reminded Nicholas of Sarah, someone who he wanted to protect, maybe I was safer than I thought I was. Still, I would give anything to have Tyler or Matt around.

Nicholas was a walking mystery. "How did you? ... you know...get turned?"

Nicholas smiled and made it all sound like it was just normal. "You know... older woman seduces boy... boy falls for her... boy gets bitten and turned into a vampire." Nicholas sounded a lot more like himself now. "Anyway, Lars and Anne are coming back tonight. If you want to wait for them with me, I will go and grab a movie or something."

I was already really tired, but I decided to wait with Nicholas anyways.

* * *

It was already past two in the morning when I woke up on the couch. The TV was off and so were most of the lights. Nicholas was nowhere in sight. I got up and went to my room. When I got there, I was so exhausted that I just flopped down on my bed and went right back to sleep.

I was abruptly woken up, but it was still so dark that I couldn't even see who it was. I knew it was a guy because of his strength. He had one hand over my mouth so I wouldn't scream, and he used his arms to keep me from moving.

The voice was not familiar at first. "Welcome, roomie," Lars said, almost in a whisper. He had a very strong European accent that made him sound even more intimidating. I did my best not to show how terrified I was which I was sure was not going well. He got closer to me. "I will make you a deal. I will turn on the lights if you promise not to scream."

I nodded.

Lars must have sensed that I wasn't lying because he did not hesitate on moving his hand away from my mouth, although he still used his arm to hold me down. He reached over me and turned on the bedside lamp. I took a deep breath and glared at him just long enough to see that his eyes were glowing red. I quickly looked away from his gaze when I realized that the reason he wanted the lights on was so that I could look into his eyes. Adrianne had once said that looking straight into a vampire's eyes was the easiest way to be glamoured, and I was sure that was what he meant to do.

I should have screamed, but I didn't. I didn't want to give him the satisfaction of knowing just how terrified I was. "What do you want?" I asked sounding much calmer than I felt.

"Let's just say it is time to collect the rent."

That is sick!

I knew very well that he was talking about my blood, and I could feel that there was a certain satisfaction in his tone. It was difficult not to look right into his eyes and tell him off, but I managed to avoid his gaze.

"Sorry to disappoint you, but you can't touch me. House rules! Now get off me," I ordered him.

Lars laughed. "So, you heard about the house rules." That wasn't so much implied as to be a question. "Here is the best part about these so called rules. My dear Anne is just so careless on her choice of words… I do believe the house rules are, the human girl stays alive and stays human."

I nodded and instantly regretted it once I realized what he meant by Anne being careless on her choice of words.

He saw it right through me. "I guess you do now realize Anne's flaw. But in case you don't, I will be specific. I can very well have my snack without killing it or changing it."

I felt cold as a shiver went through my body, but without Tyler around to protect me, I was beginning to react a little better to these situations. I shoved his arm off me, got up, and quickly ran towards the door. Unfortunately, I couldn't move quickly enough to outrun a vampire. Screaming would probably have been better than trying to outrun him, but now, screaming was no longer an option.

Lars held me against the wall with a tight grip around my neck. I wasn't able to get one word out. I felt the pressure of his nail scratching my shoulder, and just when I felt the blood running down my skin, I glanced at him and noticed his eyes were glowing brighter.

He got closer.

In a blur of movements Lars let go of my neck as Nicholas pulled him back.

Nicholas was stronger and didn't struggle at all. Nicholas didn't say one word to Lars, but Lars on the other hand was cursing as he was being dragged out of my room.

I had both of my hands clasped around my neck which I was sure was probably already bruised.

Nicholas stopped at the door not for a moment letting go of Lars' neck. He glared at my shoulder. Sounding uncomfortable and annoyed, he said, "Clean that up, or I cannot guarantee that I can keep myself from finishing what he started."

Chapter 5

That night, the house was so silent; it was as if no one was there but me. Still, I could not bring myself to step outside of my room. Honestly, even though my shoulder was no longer bleeding, I was even afraid of opening the door to Nicholas; afraid that he would still be able to pick up a scent of my blood.

I had my bedroom door locked, knowing very well that was not enough to keep a vampire out.

I couldn't sleep and I couldn't find a thing to keep me occupied.

I went to the bathroom, where the lighting was better and I would be able to better assess the damage to my neck and shoulder. Luckily, I could get to the bathroom from my room; it only made sense that I had the room with the bathroom, considering that the others didn't exactly need a bathroom… as far as I was aware of.

The bathroom was gigantic! It had a full size mirror, and the lighting… well, now that I actually saw how badly I looked, I wished the lighting in the bathroom wasn't that good after all. The lack of sleep was starting to show. My neck was already turning all shades of purple and then there was that scratch on my shoulder, which looked the least worse of all, it actually looked like a thin paper cut…. but my neck! I was so frustrated that I actually made a fist with my hand and smashed it against the mirror.

The clicking sound startled me, I was already expecting the mirror to fall forward and was ready to catch it, but instead, the mirror slowly started to open into the wall, as if it was a door into another room…and so it was.

Inside, the lighting was just as poor as in the other rooms… but there was something different about this room; it was warm. This room was surrounded by bookshelves, and in the back of the room there was a desk, like an office desk, but this one looked ancient, made with white marble that matched the bookshelves. The entire room was just beautiful and peaceful.

I started scanning through the bookshelves and there were a lot of books that I had read, mostly for school. Some books were more recent than others, like Stephen King books, and then in the back of the room, behind the desk, there was a bookshelf that wasn't as organized as the others. The books seemed older. I grabbed one of them, the year was 1864, hand-written, and the title was 'Imprints'.

I suddenly heard a noise that I couldn't even recognize where it was coming from. I instantly took that book and went the same way I came in, slowly closing the mirror once I stepped back into my bathroom, and then walking into my room.

It turned out that the book was actually a journal that seemed to contain findings about the works of a blood imprint. It was actually difficult to read, not just because of the handwriting, but also for the fact that the book had been damaged with age.

I still had a few hours before I would need to get ready for school, and I sure could not go to sleep, not that night, so I just sat on my bed and started to read it.

Overall, the book, well…the journal, was very well organized, which helped me skip to the parts that I was curious about. I could always go back and read the rest later. One thing I had been curious about was the breaking of an imprint. I knew Tyler had done it, I just didn't know how, and this hadn't been the first time. After Tyler drank my blood, I could sense his mood, but ever since he attempted to erase my memory, which was still painful just to think about him doing that, well, ever since then, I could not sense him anymore.

I found that section of the journal and it was mostly about

imprints between vampires, how bound and eternal that was, and then, there was one entry about breaking human imprints and it stated that it was almost impossible to break a blood imprint with a human. Once a vampire drank from a human, the vampire would be able to sense that human for as long as the human was alive. Humans weren't however bound to the same standards. A vampire could simply bite and drink from another human or even from another vampire and the human that was previously bitten should no longer feel the imprint; the imprint would be broken, fading over time. It was noted that in that case the vampire drained and killed the next human that he bit, to prevent that human to feel the imprint. So, that vampire could still sense the first human who he or she had imprinted with, but the human couldn't.

I clasped my hands over my mouth. Tyler can still sense me. And then I could feel the tears coming. It became even more painful knowing that wherever Tyler was he could sense me, know that I was in danger and terrified, and still not be around; not to mention that he had to have drunk someone's blood for me to stop sensing him… and this had not been the first time. Once before, I stopped sensing Tyler, and he said that he had felt that same distance, he had lied. I now sat there trying to convince myself that he had done it to protect me, but that wasn't going well. It didn't take long to get that thought out of my head and blame myself for everything. He probably just didn't want to be around. The first thing that I did when I learned Matt was still around was push Tyler away, even if I just needed time to think things through… It was painful to realize this, but I knew that I was at fault. I pushed Tyler away.

I wiped the tears and continued reading the journal. The following page explained how to use an imprint to call on one another. Those were just vampire-to-vampire imprints, but I wondered if it would work on the human-to- vampire cases as well. It explained step-by-step how to just use your mind, focus on that person, visualize your surroundings as you call their name, and ask them to come to you. According to the notes, that bond was just as strong as the bond between a vampire and his maker, and close to impossible to refuse the calling. I quickly closed the book and put it away, there was no way I even going to attempt it. Tyler probably didn't want to be around and that just felt like obligating him to come back.

There was a knock on the door. "Lexi, it is Nicholas. Can I come in?"

I made sure the book was put away where he could not see it and opened the door.

Nicholas rolled his eyes, "Again with the crying?"

I shrugged.

"We are leaving for school in about 10 minutes. You look awful! Did you get any sleep?"

I shook my head. I hadn't even realized what time it was. "Thanks for letting me know I look awful, that always helps," I said in a sarcastic tone. "I think I'm just going to stay home today."

He sighed. "Fine, but don't make this a habit, don't want your parents getting mad at me. And don't even think about leaving the house. I will know if you do and trust me, I will find you."

Anne came in, pushing Nicholas out of the way. She rolled her eyes at him. "Oh please, Nicholas! She is eighteen, I think she can decide things on her own."

Just the sight of her made me feel cold and empty. Anne looked different than any other vampire I had ever seen, I was never this up close to her before, but... well, she was as pale as they all were, she had short, shoulder-length black hair, but her eyes were different from the others; they were green, just looked…human, not the usual dark, golden or red eyes that all vampires seemed to have. She also looked very… angelic, which made me think of the wings I thought I had seen on her before… but right now, there were no signs of anything, and that didn't seem like something anyone would be able to hide, so, yeah, I had clearly been imagining things.

The one thing that bothered me the most about Anne was her familiar scent. The intoxicating scent that I recall from my childhood memories of this woman who I could only describe as a guardian angel, but even though the scent was familiar and related to good memories, all I could sense around Anne was evil.

Anne sat on my bed, clearly making herself comfortable. She might have looked angelic, but her tone was cold and direct. "Hello. As you probably already guessed, I'm Anne. I want to welcome you to the house and apologize for Nicholas' behavior. I made the necessary adjustments to the house rules. No one bites you and no one drinks blood from you in any possible way. That should cover everything, yes?"

The way she said that made it seem like she was talking about a house rule as simple as … I don't know, not eating each other's food, not as if that would apply to this particular situation; although, I guess in this house I could have been considered food… Just the thought of that made me shiver.

I barely nodded in agreement to the house rules, as she was already walking out of my room, calling Nicholas and Lars to get in the car so they wouldn't be late for school.

* * *

Knowing that I was alone in the house made me feel better. I was exhausted and whether I wanted to or not, I needed sleep, badly. I locked my door and lay down on my bed under the comforter. I wished at least my room was as warm as that secret room, which I wasn't sure whether to call it an office or our own personal library, I mean, there were thousands of books in there. That secret room was just so warm that I even thought about going in there and setting up a sleeping bag on the floor, but I was afraid there were other hidden entrances leading there besides the one through my bathroom.

I didn't wonder about that much longer, I fell asleep. I dreamed about walking into that same room, the secret room that I was thinking about before I fell asleep. It felt warm, calm, and safe. I lay down on the soft carpet, right in the center of that room; I closed my eyes and focused on the image of Tyler. I went into deep thought, reliving the intimate moment when he had drunk my blood, then I visualized where I was, and subconsciously started calling out his name.

I woke up, saying his name out loud. I frantically looked around and I was in my room, but that didn't make me feel any better. That dream had been too real. What have I done? I ran to my desk, grabbing the journal about imprints that I still had in my room, scanning through the pages, and there didn't seem to be anything about being able to call on a vampire from a dream, but then again, most of the stories in that journal were vampire-to-vampire imprints and vampires didn't sleep, therefore, they didn't dream.

I did the only thing I could think of. I sat down, closed my eyes, took a few deep breaths, focused on Tyler and told him not to come. The problem was… I didn't mean a word of what I was saying.

Chapter 6

I was just falling back asleep when my cell phone rang. I glanced at the screen, but I didn't recognize the number, so I just put it on vibrate and went to sleep.

A couple of hours later I got up, starving. I went straight to the kitchen, grabbed a sandwich and a coke, and went back to my room. I felt a lot better now that I had gotten some sleep. I was half way done with my sandwich when I heard my phone vibrating on the nightstand. I went and got the phone, it was that number again, the one I did not recognize, so I just ignored the call. That was when I realized how many missed calls I had.

I just stared at my phone in shock… over ten missed calls, all from that same number, only one voice mail…

"Alexis, this is Adrianne. I know you are not answering because you are mad at me, but please put that aside for now and at least call me back." Adrianne left her cell phone number, which she had changed, probably to avoid me in case my memory returned.

Adrianne was right, I was mad at her, but I called her anyways. If me calling on Tyler from that dream had really worked, I wanted to be able to stop him from coming to me out of pure obligation.

She answered the phone on the first ring.

"Lexi?"

"Hi Adrianne."

"I'm so glad you called. Look, I know you are mad, but we had to leave, there was no other option."

"Yeah, I thought you would say that. So, how exactly did you figure out that I regained my memory?"

Adrianne took a long pause. "Tyler called. He said somehow he felt called towards you, but he is too far away to get to you right away. He is really worried… and he has reason to be."

"Where is he? … Never mind, I don't need to know that. I didn't really mean to call on him or whatever it was I did."

"So, you did call on him?" She asked.

"No… I mean, yes, but I didn't mean to. Sorry, but he really doesn't have to come. He did his best to make me forget him and I don't want him to feel obligated to come back. Besides, I'm fine. No reason for him to be worried."

"You think you are fine?! Alexis, I had to pull some strings with your mom's job to get their phone number. Then, I called her, and found out that not only you stayed in New York, but you are living with Nicholas, Lars and Anne?!"

I lifted my hand up, barely touching the scratch on my shoulder and thought about Nicholas, so that what I was saying wouldn't be a complete lie. "It is not that bad, Adrianne. They are fine. They won't hurt me."

"So there is no way I can talk you into leaving that house? And why aren't you in school today anyways?"

"I didn't feel well today and no, I'm not moving out."

Adrianne sounded frustrated. "Fine, Lexi, I guess you leave me no other option, I'm on my way."

I kind of did want to see Adrianne, so I didn't stop her. "Do as you please, Adrianne. Where are you coming from, just so that I know when to expect you?"

"It will only be a few hours. I'm in Manhattan. Tyler will be much longer though, he is overseas with Loren, and well, that is complicated."

"Adrianne, I know you will come no matter what I say, and that is fine. At least this way you will see that I'm safe; that there is nothing to worry about, but please don't tell Tyler where exactly I'm living or that he needs to come."

Adrianne paused. "Uh-huh. I'm not going to make any promises, Lexi. I will call you when I get close to the house. Maybe we can meet somewhere."

"About that, I kind of made a deal with Nicholas that I only go out when he is around. He is really good to me, I kind of owe him that."

"Jeez, Lexi! I will just call you when I get there, we will figure something out."

* * *

I was in the kitchen, cleaning up my dishes when Nicholas walked in.

"Hey. I got your school work; I will go over everything with you."

Nicholas was in every single one of my classes, which could be annoying at times, but I guess he meant well and I could have used his help, but I wasn't sure if I should tell him about Adrianne coming, so I figured it was best to just keep a little distance for now.

"It is alright, I got it. I will come get you if I need help." Before he could get a chance to disagree, I changed the subject. "Where are Lars and Anne?"

"No clue. They dropped me off and took the car. Anyway, I will be in my room if you need me."

Nicholas was just about to step out of the kitchen when he stopped, turned around and said, "Oh, and before I forget... You are welcome to have company over whenever you would like to, as long as you know that moving out is not an option. And let your friends know that if they try and take you, there will be consequences, and don't be ... well don't take your human feelings out on me. This came from Anne."

Ugh. He knows about Adrianne. Wonderful! "How did you know...?"

He shrugged. "I know stuff... Are we clear on the no-moving-out situation?"

It was annoying that sometimes, he talked to me as if I was a prisoner, but he was right. I couldn't really go anywhere...I knew too much. "Where else would I go?" I asked, in a sarcastic tone.

"Exactly." Nicholas smiled and left the kitchen.

* * *

Adrianne called a few hours later. She was in town and wanted to know if I had figured out what we were going to do about getting together. She sounded surprised and nervous when I asked her to come to the house.

"Wonderful! I will be there in a few minutes, but please come to the door if you can. I would rather not come across any of your roommates just yet."

I agreed. Adrianne said she was only a few minutes away, which in vampire time probably meant seconds away, so I went to the door. As I came down the stairs, Nicholas was going back to his room with some girl who I had never seen. He could be such a jerk sometimes, but at least I knew he would be busy for a while. Anne and Lars were still not back and I hoped they would not return any time soon.

It was good seeing Adrianne. Good, but weird. I wished I could act like nothing had happened, like I wasn't mad at all, but that was far from the truth.

Adrianne seemed distant. She was tense and not in her usual cheerful mood.

We went to my room and as soon as I closed the door, Adrianne let out the questions.

"Alexis, what in the world happened to your neck?"

Oh boy! So I had forgotten to wrap a scarf around my neck and she could see all of the bruises.

"Oh, this was nothing, just a little incident." I shrugged.

She rolled her eyes, clearly aware that I was lying. "Alright, we were afraid that you might be in danger when we found out that you never moved back to Florida, but did you have to move into the house with the ones who are a threat to you?" Adrianne shook her head in disbelief.

She also looked sad, sounding almost heartbroken as she said, "You know... I can't protect you, not like Tyler can. Right now he is trying to get Loren to let him come here."

"You told him?!"

"Yes, I told him, even though you could say that he already had an idea of where you were...I mean, you did call on him."

"But I don't need him to come. I called on him from a dream, that shouldn't even have worked. Either way, I'm fine Adrianne. Nicholas is not that bad."

Adrianne laughed, an odd laugh considering her sad eyes. "You may even be right about that, but the girl... Anne, you need to watch your back around her. She is different."

"Different how?"

“That is what I’m trying to find out. In the mean time, would you please allow Tyler around you or at least move somewhere safer?”

I missed Tyler terribly, but I still didn’t know what to do about him and Matt being around, and it was just not fair to keep him around if I wasn’t sure about anything. Not to mention that I was still full of anger because of what he had done.

“I appreciate your concern, Adrianne, but I need to live my own life. I’m here merely because I know too much, so as long as they know they can trust me, I will be fine. And as far as Tyler is concerned, I don’t want him around. I can’t trust someone who did what he did, and I’m not talking just about messing with my memory. I also know that he broke the blood imprint by drinking blood from someone else.”

Adrianne met my gaze sounding surprised that I knew that, but mostly she seemed annoyed. “He did what he had to protect you, but now… it would be just easier if you allow him to protect you, he thinks he owes you at least that much. Do you understand it? He wants you to trust him again, to feel safe around him. He is not going to be hiding outside or secretly following you. Without your consent to be around he will stay away.”

“Good,” I said the word not really meaning it. I guess even though Nicholas wasn’t that bad, until I got over what Tyler did, I hoped he would try to be around even without me knowing about it, still protecting me, which made me feel like a horrible person for not knowing what to do about him and Matt.

Adrianne was not happy. She said she would come check on me once again in a few hours, before she left to go out of town.

* * *

It was dawn when Adrianne came back. She walked in and woke me up. She threw her designer handbag on a chair next to my bed and crossed her arms. She was also stomping her foot. She was furious!

"I hope you are happy!" She said in a cold tone.

I was in disbelief that Adrianne was capable to get this mad. I sat up on my bed, trying to fully wake up.

"How did you get in here?"

"Front door. Had to wait for your roomies to go fetch their dinner."

"What is going on?"

"Jeez, Lexi, I don't think you realize how much that boy loves you."

"I think I do, and apparently not enough to keep a promise." Okay, that was a little harsh.

"Fine. If I need to break this down for you, I will play your little game. He said if he can't protect you he would find someone who can."

"So what, he asked Loren for help?"

Adrianne shook her head in disbelief, and then met my gaze.

"I wish it was as simple as that. Loren forbade him to come around you, but disobeying his maker's order is not the worst of it. I swear, boys get even dumber when they are in love," she said in an upset and sarcastic tone.

I looked at her confused.

"Lexi, Tyler went to look for Matt."

"Oh."

"Oh?! That is not even the worse part! ... I tried to reason with him. Told him that it wasn't going to do any good because even if he can find Matt and get past Scarlett to get Matt over here, Matt cannot protect you during the day."

Without allowing me time to react she continued.

"Then, that fool... you know, Tyler, not the other fool who tried to turn you right at the beach...well, anyway, that fool actually said that he will allow Matt to drink from him, drink enough to where his blood will allow Matt to be like us during the day and so that he will be able to control Matt enough to keep him from turning you."

I clasped both hands over my mouth. "Doesn't that mean they will... "

Adrianne finished my sentence. "Imprint?"

She laughed and she was even more furious now. "Yes, and guess what?! This is the worst type of imprint. Do you want to know why?"

I nodded, avoiding her gaze.

"Because they both love you, Lexi. And being into each other's heads like that...whether they kill each other or kill themselves, this will not end well. And yes, there are ways to get a vampire killed but no human need to know about that, so don't even ask me." That had been the first time Adrianne talked to me like I was inferior to her, and that was painful, but this was my fault, and before I could even begin to apologize, she cut me off.

"... and now I have to go and try to stop Tyler before he does anything stupid."

I met her gaze. "He won't find Matt. Even Nicholas doesn't know where he is."

Adrianne shook her head. "Oh please, Lexi, Nicholas is only trying to help himself."

"That meaning?"

"That meaning he is a selfish bastard. Why would he help you find Matt?"

"Fine, then if you think Tyler will find Matt, I will go with you to find them both."

"Oh, you are definitely not going!"

I looked down. I knew I would only get in her way and make things worse.

"What about Loren, could he help?"

"Are you even listening? That night, after the incident at the beach, Loren ordered Tyler to stay away from you and told Tyler he would be required to accompany him to a trip overseas. And by the way, Loren was the reason Tyler tampered with your memory."

She sighed, and then continued.

"Tyler said he just couldn't bare the thought of you thinking that he left you. Persuaded by Loren, he convinced himself that by erasing certain things around your memory of us, of our kind, he would lessen the risks brought by your knowledge."

Now I felt horrible. "Can we at least try to call Tyler, tell him to come back, that I'm fine with him protecting me?"

Adrianne seemed to be a little calmer now. “Not even worth a try, he will think we are tricking him into coming back to change his mind.

Adrianne left in that same bad mood, leaving me afraid for Tyler and completely helpless.

Chapter 7

Tyler

Tyler was able to return from overseas a lot quicker than he expected, and he didn't have to look for Matt. He knew where to find Matt's maker, Scarlett, and that was enough.

Scarlett lived underground in one of the oldest libraries in Manhattan. Although this wasn't like any other underground location, it was actually well lit, mostly by candles and it was well furnished; furniture that consisted mostly of antiques.

She was there waiting for Tyler when he arrived, almost as if she knew he would be coming, and her mischievous smile made it seem like she knew the exact reason for his visit.

Scarlett did have plenty of reason to smile. Tyler made an offer that was very tempting; he offered to trade himself, his devotion and services in exchange for Matt's freedom. Matt was also in that same room, sitting by her side, but he seemed to be under some kind of spell. He didn't move, he didn't blink, he certainly didn't breathe but he had no need to... he was just there, staring into space.

Scarlett seemed to think over Tyler's proposal for a while. "Oh dear! This sure is tempting." She paused and licked her lips, as she looked him over. "Unfortunately, I'm afraid my dear Matthew is much more fun. He enjoys hunting as much as I do. He is good company. From what I hear you feed off some sort of plastic bag with donated blood. That does not seem very appetizing... I'm afraid your diet will not fit in with my lifestyle."

Tyler looked disappointed. He didn't know any other way to protect Lexi from this world he had exposed her to. He felt as if he was running out of time and out of options.

It was painful for him to say his next words, but for the first time in his life...well, existence, he found himself begging for help, and even worse, help from someone he could not stand for some reason.

Scarlett looked him over once again. "Very well, I will make you a deal. I really enjoy having company, so stay with us for a while, at least for a drink, and if my dear Matthew decides that he wishes to leave with you, he may do so."

The deal sounded too good to be true, and Tyler was well aware of that, but he didn't believe he had any other options.

They walked towards the area in which there was a dining set. Scarlett sat at the head of the table, Matt sat to her right and she motioned for Tyler to sit to her left.

A young girl who didn't look a day over fifteen came in carrying a tray with three wine glasses and placed them on the table. She was also a vampire, but she looked as if she was terrified. Not once did she even look up to meet any of their gazes. At Scarlett's dismissal, the girl quickly returned to where she came from.

In the wine glasses, there was blood, which surprised Tyler considering that Scarlett had just made fun of him for drinking from a blood donation bag. But he could smell the sweet scent of the blood...it was fresh.

Tyler was confused when Scarlett moved her hands towards the top of the table, asking them to join her and pray.

There was no hesitation from Matt, who had yet to say anything, but as soon as Tyler touched Scarlett's hand, whatever spell Matt was under had now been broken. He looked angry.

Neither Matt nor Tyler could move. Scarlett had her eyes closed but she was still smiling. Tyler had lost control of everything including his thoughts, but he was able to quickly figure out what Scarlett was doing. She was controlling his mind, and through her touch, she was allowing Matt to get into Tyler's mind to see and feel everything that happened on every single encounter that Tyler and Lexi had. Matt had always known that things had happened between Tyler and Lexi, but he wasn't fully aware to what extent; he wasn't aware of how strong her feelings for Tyler were.

Once it was over, Matt was even angrier. There were no signs of emotional pain, only jealousy. Matt brutally let go of Scarlett's hand and reached across the table, grabbing Tyler by his neck.

Scarlett interrupted. "Let go, Matthew. I think I had enough entertainment for the evening."

Tyler knew how big of a mistake this had been, and Scarlett chose her words carefully when rushing Matt to make his choice.

"My dear Matthew, I made Tyler a promise and now you must choose. Do you wish to leave with our friend?"

Matt didn't even answer. He turned around and went towards the same direction that the young girl had entered and left the room minutes before.

Tyler sat there frozen, feeling even worse now that he had been manipulated in such a way, but he wasn't going to confront Scarlett. He knew all too well that she was older, stronger and overall more powerful.

Scarlett met his gaze. "I do believe Matthew has made his choice. You may go now, but please come back to visit. This was very…entertaining."

Tyler bowed and turned to leave when Scarlett's cold words stopped him.

"Before you go, there is something that just crossed my mind... If you really wish to have Matthew, there is something that you could do for me." Tyler knew this had trap written all over it but he listened. "You see, Loren Crowel has something that belongs to me and I would like returned."

"What would that be?" Tyler asked in a tone that was just as cold.

"Adrianne. She was my property once before. I would like to have her back."

Tyler stood there in shock as he realized that Scarlett was Adrianne's maker. She was the one responsible for Adrianne's painful memories that were many up until Loren traded a favor in exchange for Adrianne, saving her from Scarlett's cruelty.

Tyler should have told her off and left, but instead, he politely nodded and walked out of the basement, disappearing into the darkness.

Chapter 8

I tried for an entire day and night to contact Adrianne, reaching only her voice mail. The agony that I felt from knowing what was possibly happening outside of this house was unbearable. If Nicholas and the others suspected anything, they kept it to themselves.

Morning came and it was time to get to school. I had already missed one day that week, and the day before, I was there, but my mind was elsewhere. Either way, I couldn't afford to miss another day, so I got up and after reaching Adrianne's voice mail once again, I forced myself to get ready for school.

Nicholas grabbed the keys, letting Anne and Lars know that he would be driving and even though my mind was mostly elsewhere, I had enough sense to call shotgun. There was just no way I was going to sit in the back with Lars or Anne, but especially Lars, who still looked at me as if I was his meal. Ew!

The ride to school was quiet. Anne, Lars and even Nicholas, kept giving each other looks as if they were speaking through their minds, which was creepy, but I had other things to worry about.

I sent Adrianne a text message letting her know that I would be in school, but for her to text me as soon as she could. She finally did text me, when I was in my third period class.

"Lexi, it is Adrianne. Can you ditch the rest of your classes and meet me somewhere?"

"Doubt it, Nicholas is in my class."

"Ok, What about next period?"

"He is in all of my classes."

"Ugh! I have Tyler. He wants to see you."

"Ok, I will come up with something. Can you pick me up in a few minutes?"

"Will do."

I started purposely coughing. "Mr. Peterson? I'm sorry to interrupt; I need to get to the nurse... I'm not feeling well."

Mr. Peterson was easy going, he was writing the pass hall note without asking anything else. Then Nicholas stood up and walked towards Mr. Peterson's desk.

"Excuse me, Mr. Peterson, she did look like she was about to pass out on her desk. Maybe I should accompany her to the nurse."

Okay, so Mr. Peterson was too laid back. He wrote Nicholas' note and sent us on our way.

"What was that all about?" I asked Nicholas, sounding as annoyed as I felt.

Out in the hall Nicholas was direct as usual. "You know that I have to go with you, right? Anne doesn't trust that guy... Tyler. And to be honest, I'm not a big fan either."

"How do you know?! You know what... Never mind. Do whatever, Nicholas. You say Anne is this and that, but you are the one hovering all the time. She is mostly gone all the time."

"I'm afraid you will find out sooner than later about Anne."

I really didn't have time for this. "Look, I'm not trying to run away, and I do believe that you have no reason not to trust me."

I wish I could have told him that I did not owe him anything, but he had saved me from Lars a few nights ago. "Can't you just let me go, just this one time?"

"Wish I could. It is not that I don't trust you… I don't trust them. I can compromise though; just make sure they take you to the house. I will follow you there and I will stay out of the way. You won't even know I'm there."

"Fine!"

"But, won't Anne and Lars need the car?"

"They will be fine," he assured me.

We walked into the nurse's office. Nicholas walked in front of me. He used his vampire ability to glamour the nurse who instantly gave us the necessary permission to leave school for the day. There were certainly benefits in being surrounded by vampires.

Adrianne was already in front of the school, waiting for me. Inside the car, there he was… Tyler. I wasn't sure how to describe his expression, he looked clearly worried, but I thought for a second that there was a hint of relief in seeing me. I sure hoped that was it because at the moment I laid eyes on him, I forgave him for everything… erasing my memory, leaving…

As I approached the car, he opened the passenger side door of my Camaro; the one he had once given me before the whole memory thing. He lifted the seat up and right before he started getting in the back seat, I noticed that his expression was consumed by pain and I remembered what Adrianne told me about him wanting to regain my trust. He truly believed I did not want him around.

"Wait," I rushed my words before he could get into the back seat. He stopped and turned around, meeting my gaze, and I just threw myself in his arms, holding him so tight that my arms were starting to feel numb. And then he whispered in my ear, "I'm so sorry, Lexi. I really couldn't… I didn't know what else to do."

Adrianne cleared her throat. "Guys, we need to go before someone from the school comes out and sees us just hanging out."

Tyler gently kissed my forehead, and then he got in the back seat. I sat in the front with Adrianne. As soon as I got in the car I could see that she was smiling. "So, where to?" She asked.

"Hmm, actually we have to go back to my house. Nicholas is following us there, but he will stay our of the way."

Neither one of them were happy about that; Adrianne was no longer smiling and looking back at Tyler through the rear-view mirror, he looked tense and annoyed.

At the house, Tyler felt uncomfortable, and he was being really quiet. I knew Nicholas wasn't too far behind us, so we all just went to my room to talk. Adrianne asked if there was anywhere we could talk and be sure that Nicholas wasn't listening, and I immediately thought of the secret room, asking them to follow me.

As I led them into the bathroom, Adrianne rolled her eyes. "Is this really your idea of a good place to talk?"

I laughed at her, and then I turned around and softly punched that spot on the mirror that opened it into the secret room.

Tyler looked at me confused. I grabbed his hand and led him inside the room. Adrianne stayed back.

"Secret room! Fancy!"

I looked back at her. "Aren't you coming?"

"No, you two need to talk. Besides, I need to stay out here in case someone comes looking for you."

I nodded and closed the mirror behind us. Inside the secret room, Tyler looked around, amused.

"How did you find this place?"

"By accident." And as soon as I said that, I thought about that night when I was so frustrated about what Lars had done to my neck and shoulder that I had hit the mirror causing that door to open, and as that memory rushed through me, I couldn't help but to touch my neck, which was still bruised. Luckily, I was wearing a scarf and Tyler couldn't see it.

Tyler came closer, locking his eyes into mine as he slowly unwrapped the scarf from around my neck. I felt an impulse to turn away from his gaze, but I just couldn't. He brushed his fingers against my neck and closed his eyes.

"I'm sorry I allowed this to happen," he said in almost a whisper.

He pulled me closer, putting his cold lips against my forehead.

"None of this is your fault, Tyler. Adrianne told me about Loren…"

"You don't need to worry about Loren, the important thing right now is that we need to get you out of here, but Adrianne seems to believe that there is something about the girl, Anne, that if we just take you out of here, it will put you in even more danger."

I met his gaze. He looked concerned.

"Anne is not just keeping me here because of what I know, is she?" I asked him, just now realizing that if that was the case, she had no reason to keep me alive.

"No." Tyler said. There has to be another reason.

I sighed. "That is what it seems, although I don't understand what she would possibly want from me."

"We don't really know either, but Adrianne is trying to find out."

"I don't think I'm in any danger, Tyler. I really don't."

His eyes turned darker. "Lexi... your neck?"

"I know, but there are house rules in place now and all. I don't want you to worry."

He didn't say anything for a few seconds.

"I'm glad you are back," I said.

That got him to smile, which made me feel so much better. I smiled right back at him and said, "I really am glad you are here."

He leaned in closer to me, closed his eyes, I closed mine, and then I felt his cold lips on mine as we kissed. He held me tighter than ever before. I felt as if he would never let me go, and I didn't want him to.

After a while, which sure didn't feel like long enough, he pulled me away slowly, held my hands, and said that he needed to regain my trust and to do that, he needed not to keep any more secrets from me.

Tyler started telling me about where he had been the evening before. He said that he had seen Matt, who was with his maker, and that she had been keeping him under some kind of spell. He told me everything, including his offer to trade places with Matt so that I would have someone's protection, and I could feel the tears rolling down my cheeks as he told me that.

He held my hands even tighter and looked into my eyes. "Lexi, I understand that you and Matt have history, but I assure you he is not whoever you used to know. Do you remember that one of the reasons I did not want to turn you was because you wouldn't be YOU anymore?" I nodded, avoiding his gaze. "Everyone changes, Lexi, and I know this will be hard for you to understand, but eventually you will realize that. I'm just not sure if I can handle waiting for that to happen, you know, if he comes back."

"I don't want you to leave, Tyler." That was all I said, although I didn't know how to feel about Matt. And I knew just how awful and selfish it was to ask Tyler to stay, especially if there was chance of Matt coming back.

Tyler sighed. "Just know that if I have to go away, it is because of Loren, but I will find my way back to you."

I crawled into his arms, feeling safe, comforted, loved … aware that some of those feelings were only temporary.

Chapter 9

Adrianne opened the mirror and her tone was tense and nervous. "You guys need to come back into the room. Now!"

Nicholas was knocking on the bedroom door and I hoped he had not been knocking for long. Adrianne tried to get Tyler to leave through the window, but he refused to. I knew that Adrianne had tried to get him to leave to avoid confrontation with Nicholas, so I glanced at Tyler, and said, "You guys can stay, but please don't start trouble. Nicholas really isn't as bad as you think."

I opened the door to find Nicholas standing there, smiling. "Thanks for the compliment, roomie," he said. Of course he had heard that.

Nicholas looked at Tyler and rolled his eyes, than he looked at Adrianne, smiled and said hello, in a very flirtatious way, which was funny because I couldn't possibly imagine that Adrianne would be dumb like his usual catches, although, the girls that he brought to the house were mostly just snacks.

Nicholas quickly interrupted my self-babbling.

"Look, Loren Crowel is downstairs, he wants the both of you (he looked at Adrianne and Tyler) to meet him there. Also, Anne and Lars are on their way."

Everyone froze in place.

There was no way around this. We all knew it. I started to make my way outside of my room when Nicholas blocked me at the door.

"Loren said to leave you up here… in his own words…'not the human girl, she must stay away'." He shrugged. "You know what, I owe him nothing. Let's go."

Downstairs, facing us, there was Loren. He looked older than I had expected, he looked as if he was in his late twenties, or maybe early thirties… He was tall, and didn't seem to be as pale as the others. He had brown hair, which looked kind of messy, but in a sexy way, his eyes were of a hazel honey color… something about him was so familiar, but I couldn't quite figure out what.

Loren looked furious.

He addressed Nicholas, but it was me that he was looking at, and I literally felt dizzy. Dizzy to the point where I lost my balance. Tyler moved to my side, supporting my weight.

"I told you to leave the human girl upstairs," he growled.

Nicholas in his sarcastic tone responded. "Oh, did you? You know, when you live as long as I have, sometimes memory just lacks…"

Loren was grabbing Nicholas by his neck when Lars and Anne came through the door at an incredible fast speed.

Lars and Anne both moved in Loren's direction. I felt Tyler flinch when he saw Lars, but I held on to his arm with a tight grip. He must have thought I was still not feeling well because he stayed where he was.

Adrianne on the other hand, moved in a blur, shoving Lars against the wall hard enough to where he just fell down and stayed there. Adrianne was now coming for Anne, but she stopped before she could get even inches closer to Anne. Adrianne, in a warning tone, said, "Loren, you need to put Nicholas down." Loren didn't move, not until he faced Adrianne's direction and actually really saw who was standing between him and Adrianne... Anne.

Anne didn't have to fight him, or even say anything. Loren let go of Nicholas, who was smiling like a fool. Loren didn't seem so confident now.

"Finally, the three of us meet again!"

Loren was tense and furious. "You! Why can't you just leave her alone?"

Anne smiled. "What, like you have?"

I whispered to Tyler. "Who are they talking about?"

Tyler shrugged. Nicholas shook his head as if I had just asked a stupid question. Adrianne looked at me in shock, and Lars just lay there, looking as if Adrianne had really hurt him.

Loren kept his gaze on Anne. "We need to talk in private."

Anne shrugged. "As you please, send your minions away."

Loren stood there, glaring at Nicholas and Lars, waiting for her to send them away first.

Anne glanced at Nicholas. "Nicholas, would you please see that Alexis gets to her room safely."

Tyler moved in front of me, blocking Nicholas from coming closer. Anne laughed. "Well, this is an interesting turn of events… your own minion, Tyler, is it?... Falling for none other than this girl."

Loren warned her. "I said, in private."

Anne faced Nicholas once again. "Would you take Alexis and her friends to her room? Just make sure they don't leave… Lars, get out of the house and go find something useful to do."

Lars went out right away, as Nicholas escorted Tyler, Adrianne and me to my room where he made himself comfortable and started to read a book, while Tyler sat by my side looking just as confused as I was, and Adrianne just looked dazed.

Chapter 10

Loren

Anne took Loren into a more private room in the house. She locked the door behind her and then, unleashed her wings.

It was difficult for Anne to transform from vampire-angel, to simple vampire form, but hiding her wings was the only way she could blend in with the humans.

Actually, hiding her wings took even more energy than letting them out, so she never allowed anyone to watch her do that. That was her one single moment of vulnerability. Keeping her wings hidden wasn't that bad, as long as it wasn't done for an extended period of time, so Anne mostly wore backless dresses and shirts, to allow room for her wings to come out through between her shoulder blades without destroying her clothes, which were her most prized possessions.

Loren looked at Anne, puzzled. "Your wings used to be white when you first fell. What happened?" Loren didn't look concerned as much as curious and afraid of what she had done, because he was right, when they first met, Anne was already a fallen angel, and even after she had been accidently turned into a vampire, her wings were white, they looked fuller, softer, and more pure. Now, all he saw was darkness.

Anne wasn't bothered by the question, she just didn't care for his thoughts and her tone reflected her lack of concern. She never once even raised her voice.

"My existence and what I do with it does not concern you, Loren. Besides, you have your own problems to worry about."

Loren knew that she had a point. "Why do you have her here, Anne?"

"Loren, you haven't changed at all...always so direct... You know, I really wished I had been there to see your reaction when you realized who she was. I actually found it quite amusing that your little human pet...what was her name? ... Right! Lydia. Anyway, she took so many centuries to reincarnate and yet, she came back looking just like she used to."

Loren was about to interrupt her, but Anne wasn't quite done, she didn't allow him to get a word in.

"... And then, fate brought her into your path by leading her into the arms of your minion. That was truly wonderful, well, to me anyways."

Loren looked annoyed and frustrated. "But why are you after this human girl now?" He couldn't even make himself say Alexis' name, almost as if that would make her more real to him. "Lydia was gone centuries ago, they are not the same person."

"Don't be a fool, Loren. Same looks, same soul, ... Alexis is Lydia."

Loren was furious, and it showed in his tone, which made Anne even more satisfied. That was one thing that made Anne stronger, she fed off other's emotions, any bad emotions...anger, depression; it all gave her a burst of energy and power.

He glared at Anne. "You haven't answered my question. What are you doing with her here? What do you want from her?"

"I have an unfinished business with her. Nothing for you to worry about."

Loren sighed; his fists were clenched, and he was really having a difficult time controlling his anger. He no longer denied who Alexis used to be. "What do you want in exchange for her?"

"Loren, you know you have nothing that I want, and don't even waste your time threatening me. You know very well that because of what I am, I'm stronger than you."

His eyes were cold. "You were supposed to protect her, Anne."

Anne smiled, an evil smile. "And I did, but look where that got me. Listen to me, Loren, what I am today, is because of the both of you... Lucky you, I'm in a giving mood today, so I will make you a deal. I give you my word that I will inflict no physical pain on the girl. Just stay out of my way and take your minions with you and I guarantee you that when I'm done with her, you and your minion can have her...all in one piece."

"What if I refuse your deal?"

"Don't be stupid, Loren. I will destroy everything close to you. The girl first and then both of your minions, and that won't even be difficult to accomplish, which is extremely annoying. I just wonder how the boy, Tyler, will react to finding out about Alexis' past life with you, and even that there is a possibility that she is only attracted to him because as your minion, he carries a part of you within him. And the girl, Adrianne, I have heard that her maker wishes to have her back."

Anne noticed Loren's hesitation.

"Ah Loren, if it ever comes to it, I don't believe you stand a chance with the girl, not with your minion, Tyler around. I honestly believe he would give his life for the girl, if that was possible. He will protect her no matter what is in his way, and that is why I need you, as his maker, to keep him away. He would not have hesitated in taking this deal, which leads me to believe that he loves her more than you ever loved her... you know... when she was Lydia."

That comment was enough to get to Loren. Anne knew exactly how to manipulate just about anyone around.

"How long do you need us to stay away?"

"Don't be so impatient, Loren. It will not take long, I assure you. I'm already getting bored with the girl. You will hear from me as soon as I'm done."

Chapter 11

I had never felt so uncomfortable in my life as I did having Nicholas, Adrianne and Tyler, all in one room, while we waited for Loren and Anne to finish talking about whatever it was that they had to talk about.

I kept expecting Tyler to get across the room and start fighting Nicholas. I didn't expect it to happen the other way around only because Nicholas was too busy attempting to flirt with Adrianne, who had been too distracted with her own thoughts to even bother telling him to leave her alone.

Tyler attempted to ask Adrianne what was going on.

Adrianne glared up at Nicholas and than met Tyler's gaze. "We will talk later."

Nicholas shook his head, and with a grin on his face, he went back to reading whatever book it was that he was reading. My heart skipped a beat when I actually focused on what he was reading. It was the journal that I had found in the secret room, the journal that had so much information about imprints.

Nicholas noticed my shocked expression and closed the book. "Pretty cool stuff in here. Where did you get it?"

"I – I got it from Adrianne," I lied.

I was glad Adrianne was so good at improvising. She quickly snapped out of her trance-like state and confirmed what I was telling Nicholas.

"Yes, it is mine, and I would like it back please… now."

I was surprised to see that Nicholas just got up, walked towards Adrianne and handed her the book. Then he sat back down on the chair. "Anne and Loren are on their way up," he said.

Anne was actually the only one to enter the room.

"Tyler, Loren would like to have a word with you," she said.

She noticed Tyler's hesitation. "Adrianne can stay with Alexis while you and Loren talk." Then she glanced at Nicholas. "You may go now. They will be alright."

Tyler waited for Anne and Nicholas to leave the room before he walked out to talk to Loren.

I really didn't feel comfortable leaving him alone with Loren, and I asked Adrianne to go after him, but she assured me that Tyler would be fine. She seemed confident as she said it, but I sensed she was not telling the truth.

"Lexi, where did you get this?" She asked, holding up the book.

"In the secret room." I was still not sure what else to call that room. "There are a lot more like this one."

"You shouldn't be reading them," she warned me.

"Yeah, I know," I agreed, even knowing that wouldn't stop me from reading them.

"Do you mind if I go look?"

I shrugged. "Knock yourself out."

"Alright, I will be quick. Just come and get me if you hear anyone coming."

I nodded, and Adrianne was gone in a blur.

I walked around in my room, very tempted to just go after Tyler, but I also didn't want anyone to walk in and get to Adrianne in that room, which I was fairly sure no one in the house knew about. I mean, they wouldn't put me in this particular room knowing there was a possibility of me finding my way in there.

Adrianne came back out within minutes; she must have known exactly what she was looking for, because she came out with a thin dark book, black cover. I was unable to see the title as she had it covered by her hand. "Do you mind if I borrow this?" Adrianne asked.

"Well, it is not mine to lend, but I really don't think anyone will miss it. What is it about?"

Before Adrianne could answer my question, Tyler was back in the room, by himself. He looked even more pale than usual.

"Adrianne, would you stay in here while I talk to Lexi?"

"Sure."

Tyler grabbed my hand and led me to the secret room.

He closed the full-size mirror that led us into the room and his eyes locked on mine. "Lexi, I have no idea what is going on here, but Loren made me an offer. He said that he needs me to go with him for a while, to do something for Anne. He said it is non-negotiable, and that while I'm gone, I will not be able to contact you in any way but that upon our return, you will be able to leave this house without any consequences."

"Did he say what her deal is? Why she wants me to stay here?"

"No. Loren said she guarantees that you will not be hurt. Who knows, maybe she just wants you to stay to make sure Loren gets done whatever it is that she wants, but I'm just guessing." Tyler took my hand in his, and I noticed for the first time, that in this room, his skin didn't feel as cold. "Lexi,

I don't like this at all. I don't want to leave you again, and I'm not sure you are as safe as Loren told me you are."

"What about Adrianne? Can she stay?"

Tyler shook his head. "No, Loren said that he needs her as well." He sighed. "It is better for Adrianne to stay away from here anyways."

"Why?" I asked.

"Lexi, I didn't tell you this before, but Matt's maker offered to trade him for Adrianne…It turns out that they have the same maker, Scarlett, and she wants Adrianne back."

I felt my stomach clench. "You are right, Adrianne needs to stay away." I knew how awful, how cruel Adrianne's maker had been to her. But now, knowing who Matt's maker was and what she was capable of doing, made me fear for him.

If Tyler felt this same fear through our imprint, he didn't say anything.

"Does Adrianne know?" I asked him.

"No, she doesn't."

I nodded, knowing it was probably better that way.

"Ty, about you having to go with Loren, just think about the outcome. When you come back, I will be able to get out of the house and go with you without having to worry about anyone coming after us… Besides, I know you don't like Nicholas, but he has been keeping me safe. The night when Lars … well… you know, my neck… Nicholas stopped him."

My words did more damage than good. Tyler's expression was overcome with pain. I don't think he meant for his words to come out, but in a whisper he said 'He protected you when I couldn't.'

"Ty, it is not like that. Besides, you are here now, and most of all, against Loren's wishes."

I saw Tyler's expression change right away. "How did you do it? How did you call me to you?"

I showed Tyler the book on imprints that Adrianne had brought back into this room and left on the table. I told him how at first, I wasn't sure if it would work, because I could feel that our imprint had faded, and that I couldn't feel him like before. I left out the part about knowing exactly how that happened…that I knew Tyler had fed from someone else.

Tyler didn't say anything about our imprint fading. He scanned through the book, smiled and said, "You know you shouldn't be reading this right? … But I'm glad you did." He pulled me closer to him and kissed me. This kiss felt different, it was more intense. It had been far too long since we were together like this. I could tell that Tyler was more relaxed and I sensed that he was up to something.

When Tyler pulled me away, he asked if I knew everything that I needed to know within that book. I nodded. I had read that book cover to cover.

"Alright, I'm going to take this with me and read it, so I know what signals to look for in case you need me. While I'm gone, if you feel like you are in any danger I want you to call me to you, just like you did the other night. I will find my way back to you."

"Ty, how will I know if something happens to you?" I said, thinking that he would need to drink from me again. That was the only way that I would be able to sense him like before.

Tyler knew exactly where I was going with that. "Lexi, I need you not to worry about me. If something happens, I will find a way to let you know, but for right now, I need you to focus on staying safe."

I nodded. "But you don't know where you are going. What if I call for you and you are too late?"

Tyler reached into his pocket. Inside it there was a gold locket necklace, with what looked like a star engraved on it. "I planned on giving this to you a while back, but Adrianne wasn't sure where it was. The five-pointed star is a symbol of protection. It doesn't seem like a lot, but it will make anyone who intends to cause you physical harm to be weak enough to where you can get away."

I doubted that a simple necklace would have such abilities, but it was beautiful. I opened the locket, and inside it, there was a really small replica of that star, but this one was silver, sharp on all ends.

Tyler smiled. "I'm not sure the locket was ever tested, so, just in case it doesn't work... If anyone tries to hurt you, just stick that through their skin, anywhere in their body. You have to make sure it is all the way in, where they cannot get to it."

I looked at him, puzzled.

"It is real silver. Yeah, I know it is so cliché, but silver does cause us pain and it destroys any vampire if they can't get rid of the silver object from within their body. Let's just hope you never need to use that."

I placed the star back in the gold locket and closed it. Then I handed Tyler the necklace and asked if he would help me putting it on.

Tyler stood behind me, moved my hair out of the way, and he put the locket necklace on. He was just about to take off the other gold necklace that I was wearing when I stopped him. I turned to face him and said, "This one stays on." Tyler softly grabbed the gold necklace, sliding his fingers over the chain, and pulling it from underneath my shirt to where he could get a full view of the necklace that had belonged to his great grandmother, a family jewel that he thought was appropriate for me to have.

He smiled.

Adrianne opened the mirror enough to say that they needed to get going, that Loren had knocked on the door and she was able to stall him for a few minutes, but he was getting impatient.

"Just a few minutes," Tyler called out.

Adrianne closed the mirror and went back into my room.

Tyler pulled me closer. "I know you have no reason to trust me, but I will find my way back to you no matter what or who is in my way."

"I do still trust you, Ty."

He whispered in my ear. "I really don't deserve you."

It was useless arguing with him, so I kissed him to shut him up, and well…because I wanted to kiss him. Besides, there was no telling when I would be able to do that again.

Chapter 12

Surprisingly enough, over the next few days, everything went back to normal, well, as normal as it could get. When we were not all in school, Anne and Lars spent most of their time outside of the house, doing who knows what… I mean… they had a really strange relationship. When I first met them, I remembered thinking of them as boyfriend and girlfriend, but now I realized that it was more like he was Anne's minion.

Nicholas, on the other hand, pretty much had his own routine. Every night, Nicholas had at least one girl over at the house. Ugh. At least they all eventually left the house, alive and in one piece, but they always acted as if everything was normal. The only reason I knew that they had been Nicholas' snacks, was because of the paper cut-like marks on their skin, which was usually on their necks. Sometimes the marks weren't visible, but I was sure they were somewhere, because those girls always looked pale when they left.

I had been paying close attention to Nicholas' routine for a while now. I knew how long the girls stayed for, so I always used that time to run into the secret room and grab one of the books from behind the desk, which were all vampire books. Sometimes, I took the risk and just read a few pages in that room. That room was just so peaceful, warm, and now, full of good memories… memories of Tyler. And since I had learned how to call Tyler to me, it was difficult not to use that knowledge just to have him around, but I was also aware that there would be consequences to my actions.

The books in that section of the room were mostly really old journals. They were all handwritten, dated back a few centuries. And I should definitely not be reading any of it, but I just couldn't stop. I even made excuses to why I should read them, like finding crucial information that could help me protecting myself.

There were so many of those journals, and I doubted I would ever finish them all, so I mostly narrowed down my search to imprints, protection and on becoming a vampire.

I had also been worried about Matt and even though I didn't know where exactly he was, other than being with his maker, Scarlett, I tried to find anything that I could use to help him. Tyler knew where they were, but when he told me that he had seen Matt, the pain in Tyler's eyes… I couldn't bring myself to ask where to find him. I did ask Nicholas if he knew where to find Scarlett, but he blew me off, saying that he didn't know and that from what he had heard, she moved around a lot anyways.

I knew that Matt's bond with his maker was strong, all vampire-maker bonds were, but I tried to find information on spells and breaking a bond between vampire and maker, which from what I had found out, could only be broken if the maker was somehow destroyed. There was however no information on destroying a vampire, probably because of the risks of the wrong person getting their hands on those journals, not that it would be good for anyone to get their hands on any of those journals either way.

I was literally amazed with the information that I had learned. In one of the books about protection, there was a picture of the same locket necklace that Tyler had given me. According to the description, the locket worked, but only against direct physical threats, and there were theories that it had to be the original locket, which belonged to a Queen in Spain, centuries back. I sure hoped I was wearing the right necklace, but most of all, I hoped that I wouldn't have to find out.

The best findings were on the imprints, it wasn't so direct to imprints, but I knew the connection had to be there. One of the journals explained that vampires could have control over a human's dream. According to the journal, it worked with any human, but I assumed that the imprint connection would probably assist in the process. Mostly, it worked as a way to relay a message to the human, and it was often used to call the human to the vampire for feeding.

That night I decided to try my own experiment. I followed the instructions from the first journal to contact Tyler. I laid down on the bed, focused on Tyler and focused on my message to him. Tyler, you can reach me through my dreams. Please try it. I miss you... I felt stupid for even thinking there was a possibility that would work, but I still hoped…

I tried to control my hopes and hold on to reality, especially after remembering that Tyler had taken that first journal so he would know what signs to look for, and there was nothing about the dream connections on that journal. Still, I was eager to fall asleep, but that night was a dreamless night.

Chapter 13

The weekend finally came, only I wasn't sure if that was a good thing or not, especially that weekend, when Anne and Lars seemed to be around more than usual. I even tried to just hang out in my room, but Nicholas basically dragged me out, he wanted to play one of his video games; said that he needed a second player and Anne and Lars were busy.

"Oh, great! So, I'm your last resort?" I asked jokingly.

Nicholas smiled. "Wow, sounds like you are finally in a good mood. Oh by the way, your parents called earlier today, said they know they are hard to reach because of work, but you should at least try calling them."

"Yeah, I know…" I was suddenly cut off on my lame excuse. I had actually tried to leave all phones unoccupied in case Tyler or Adrianne called, even though Ty said they wouldn't be able to.

We heard a knock on the front door and I instantly felt anxious, which was odd, considering that we were not expecting anyone. I walked towards the door but before I was even halfway there, Nicholas met my gaze and walked, well, walked at a vampire speed that would be considered running to any human, towards the door. "Stay back!" he ordered me, in a tone that indicated there was danger ahead.

When Nicholas opened the door and I saw who was there, my knees instantly felt weak. I missed him terribly and my urge to get closer was immediate but my gut feeling that something was not right quickly overshadowed it.

At first, Matt didn't even look at me. His gaze was locked on Nicholas'. The worse part of it all was that I had been around them, vampires, long enough to know that Matt had just fed, besides, I could smell it, he reeked of blood.

Matt sounded confident and just…different. "Aren't you

going to invite me in, dude?" Matt glanced at me, and then at Nicholas. His words confirmed my suspicions that something was wrong. That was not the Matt I knew and loved. "I see you have something that belongs to me."

Nicholas just shook his head and laughed. "Man, how many times did you feed today?"

"A few."

"Scarlett really does let her own run loose at feeding time, doesn't she?"

Matt looked as if he was losing his patience. "Are you inviting me in or not?"

Nicholas almost did invite him in, but then he realized that I was still there. When Matt noticed Nicholas' hesitation he looked at me.

Nicholas, also looking at me said, "Lexi, do not look into his eyes."

But just the sound of Matt's voice seemed to be enough to get to me. His tone had changed to the old Matt, the one I knew and couldn't live without. I also knew that because of the imprint, Tyler could still feel what I felt, and I hoped he did not link it to Matt being back. To say that I was confused about Ty and Matt was an understatement.

"Lex, babe, I miss you. I just want to talk. Invite me in." Dazed, I was just about to invite him in when my trance-like state was broken off by the sound of Anne's voice as she came down the stairs.

"Don't be rude, Nicholas. Invite the boy in."

Nicholas didn't say a word.

Anne rolled her eyes at Nicholas and pushed him out of the way as she approached the door. Anne looked Matt up and down and licked her lips, "You must be Matt. Please come in."

The way Anne acted made me feel… well; jealous enough to put my gut feeling aside and move towards him, but Nicholas stopped me. He came closer and whispered, "Don't! He is under the influence of more things than you can possibly imagine. Keep your distance and stay where I can see you."

Anne heard him. "She is not your pet, Nicholas. No need for the additional protection. She is home, she is safe enough." Then she looked at Matt, "I assume you are here to see Alexis, yes?"

Matt went back to avoiding my gaze. The one time he did glance at me, I could sense anger. Why is he so angry? Is he angry with me? He quickly went back to looking at Anne, and said, "I also need a place to stay for a while."

"What about Scarlett?" Nicholas asked.

"She is taking care of some personal affairs, she will be gone for a while. No need to bother her," he said, in a warning tone.

"No need to explain yourself," Anne said, and she continued as if I was not even there. "You may stay, but we have one condition, well a few conditions really… Alexis stays human, no one feeds from her, and she stays in this house. You so much as try to turn her or take her away and I will personally make sure that Scarlett is informed and you never see Alexis again. Is that understood?"

Matt agreed, but I could tell his words meant nothing. He may have looked like a whole new person, but his expression was just the same as when he used to lie to his parents about being at a friends' house for the weekend, when we were actually spending the weekend together.

I noticed that Nicholas had his fists clenched. "Where do you suppose he stays, Anne? We only have four rooms."

"Don't be rude, Nicholas. He can share a room with one of us, well, except for Alexis of course. Well, now that I think about it, neither you nor Lars like sharing your personal space either… hmm."

Did she just suggest that Matt shares the room with her?!

Nicholas grabbed my wrist, stopping me from reacting in any way. He met Anne's gaze. "Anne, why don't you show Matt the rest of the house and what rooms to stay out of, while Alexis and I finish the game."

Anne agreed. She actually seemed eager to do so.

Nicholas put his finger over his lips as to warn me not to say anything and minutes later, when he was sure that Anne was far away enough to where she couldn't hear us, he looked at me and said, "You may not want to tell Anne off or disagree with her, that will just entice her in provoking you more and more."

I was frustrated… very frustrated. "Why is she doing this?"

Nicholas shrugged. "Does it really matter, Lexi? Aren't you back-together with that other dude?"

Ouch. Okay, he was right about that, but that didn't keep me from caring about Matt. "What is going on with Matt, why is he acting like that?"

"Over-eating."

I looked at him like he was crazy.

"I'm serious, Lexi. Bloodlust – fastest way to wiping your humanity away."

Chapter 14

Anne and Matt walked back in the room, both laughing and in general, in a good mood. Matt still wouldn't even look at me. He asked Nicholas what game he was playing, as if I wasn't even there and still holding the game controller. But that got Nicholas to go on and on about the game. Anne and I just watched them talking. Anne just looked bored, and I kept wondering how to fix whatever was wrong with Matt, wondering if there was even a cure for bloodlust? Which from what Nicholas said, was almost like a virus that was taking away his humanity.

* * *

I always knew when Nicholas or the others had just fed, and that glow in their eyes, which gave it away, would always last for at least a day or so. When that glow vanished and their eyes got either darker, or turned into a glowing red, depending on their mood, it was the first sign that they were hungry. That was how I knew when to stay even further away as possible from Lars.

With Matt, that glow was vanishing faster. I knew that he had recently fed, probably right before he got to the house. According to Nicholas, Matt had fed several times that evening. Yet, his eyes were darker than any other vampire I had ever seen.

I noticed a glimpse of that darkness when he first stopped avoiding looking at me, although at that moment, I caught myself wishing that he was still ignoring me.

Lars looked at me like this before, when he wanted to drink my blood, only Matt's glare was much more intense. He didn't see me anymore. To him, I was nothing more than a blood bank.

That was painful. I literally felt the pressure of the pain on my chest. I tried to avoid feeling like that, mostly because I didn't want to put Tyler through feeling what was happening to me, and I knew that because of our imprint, he would, but I couldn't help it.

The effects of Matt's last feeding were fading, and so fast... his thirst was becoming unbearable, and he was losing control. I was afraid that Anne's rules would not be enough to keep him from hurting me, and I put my hand over the necklace that Tyler gave me for protection, hoping that would work. Matt wouldn't hurt me. I kept telling myself, although I did not believe my own words. I wasn't sure I would even be able to make myself get away if anything happened.

Matt made a cautious movement towards me. Anne wasn't trying to stop him, at least not yet; in fact, she was smiling in a creepy way.

"Lexi, let's go," Nicholas said, in a very urgent tone.

I couldn't move. My body felt limp. Nicholas walked towards me and pulled me up by my hand and started to lead me upstairs.

Anne glared at Nicholas, and she was clearly annoyed.

As I looked back before going upstairs, I saw Anne asking Matt to sit back down, then she placed her hands on his shoulders, which I wasn't sure if it was to keep him down or just to touch him, but that made me want to go back and stay there. I didn't know what she was up to, but I had to find a way to keep Matt away from her. Just the thought of them around each other made my stomach clench.

* * *

"So, can't Matt just share the room with you?" I asked Nicholas in a desperate tone.

"Not a chance!"

"But, it is not like you sleep, right? So why do you even need a room anyways?"

Nicholas seemed annoyed with the begging.

"You know, for a smart girl, you sure ask a lot of questions. You should have known by now that some things are just better left alone…but I'm sure you won't leave it alone, so let's just say that most of us like to have our meals in private."

The image of Nicholas feeding on the girls he brought to his room flashed through my mind. Ew. Okay, I shouldn't have asked.

"Anne doesn't seem to have an issue with such privacy!"

"Anne is not like most of us," he snarled. He sounded frustrated as if there was something about Anne I had yet to notice. Then, he closed his eyes and sighed, as if trying to calm down.

Anne knocked on my bedroom door. At least she knocked.... "Nicholas, I need to have a word with you. Now!"

Nicholas rolled his eyes and went out of my room to talk to Anne, closing the door behind him.

Anne must have forgotten that although as a human, I lacked their more developed hearing; I was not deaf, because I was sure she didn't think I could hear her from inside my room.

It sounded like she had slammed Nicholas against the wall, and it was with such a force that made the wall vibrate and one of my picture frames which was hanging on the wall fell, and I could hear her every word. She sounded calm, yet threatening.

"Do not cross me Nicholas! … You know I'm stronger and I will crush you. I don't care what your reason is for trying to protect your little pet, and I'm sure it is a disturbing one, but if you cross me again, there will be consequences.... If I believe that she is in danger with the boy, I will personally intervene... besides, she has the necklace; she will be fine."

I instantly put my hand over the locket necklace that Tyler gave me.

How does she know?

It was silent after that. Nicholas didn't come back to my room. I sure wasn't stupid enough to open the door and go looking for him, so I just went to bed.

* * *

That Saturday morning, I got up, and was just about to get out of my room when I saw a note under my door. It was from Nicholas.

Hey Lexi,

Anne, Lars and I are out for the day. No need to worry about Matt, he needs complete darkness during the day, so he will surely stay put where he is.

PS: Don't do anything stupid. We will be back before dark.

Nicholas

I got out of my room, planning on getting some breakfast, calling my parents and then taking advantage of the fact that I was home alone and go into the secret room.

On my way down the stairs, I walked by Anne's bedroom door and I realized what Nicholas meant by me not doing anything stupid. I stopped in front of that door, wondering what Matt was doing. He was different than all of the others I had met so far. Besides not being able to control his bloodlust,

Matt couldn't go out during the day. Seemed like quite a few vampires couldn't, unless they came from certain families or drank from the ones who could go out in daylight; it was something to do with their blood... what exactly, I had yet to find out.

I wondered if Matt maybe slept during the day, or if he just hid in the dark doing nothing.

I scared myself when I realized that my hand was already touching the doorknob to open the door. Anne had always locked her door, I tried to sneak in before and that was how I knew it, but just the fact that I was somehow lured into trying to open that door terrified me.

I quickly pulled my hand away from the doorknob, ran downstairs and went for a walk.

I walked to the closest restaurant, called my parents while I ate, then I went to a bookstore where I got a book and a few magazines and went home.

Only, when I got to the house, I couldn't find the courage to go in. I knew I would be tempted to open that door, so I went around to the backyard. Sat down on the back porch and started scanning through the magazines I had just bought, realizing how long it had been since I went shopping and how badly I needed new clothes and shoes, and...

I felt as if someone was watching me. I looked around and there was no one. When I glanced behind me and up, I realized that Anne's window faced the backyard, but the blinds were closed, there was nothing to see... and then I saw the blinds moving.

Chapter 15

"Bloodlust – the disease that makes us the monsters we are known to be; it is what wipes away the last of our humanity."

That was on the very first page of one of the oldest journals that I had found in the secret room.

After feeling as if I was being watched while I sat outside in the back yard, I decided to take the risk and run to the one place where I felt safe. So I ran upstairs and straight to my room, without even stopping to look at Anne's bedroom door. I knew if I had stopped I would have been tempted to go in.

I walked into my room, then went into the bathroom, locked the door and turned the shower and the radio on, so that anyone who might have come to look for me would think that I was in the shower. I then pressed the spot on the right hand corner of the full-size mirror, which opened right away, and I walked into the secret room, finding what seemed to be the only journal that referenced bloodlust. At times, it was almost as if something in that room wanted me to find the exact journals that I was looking for. There were just so many of them, yet, somehow I was always able to find the right one.

The journal described bloodlust exactly as I had imagined, a virus, eating away someone's humanity. I searched for hours for the cure, but there had yet to be one. According to the journal, bloodlust came with their lifestyle. Some of them would be able to control it, like Tyler. For others, it was just a matter of accepting their fate. The worst part was that bloodlust wasn't so much about the thirst or hunger as it was about an uncontrollable desire to hunt and hurt their prey. The author of that journal made it very clear on his beliefs that in reality, none of it mattered. According to his beliefs, they became soulless at the moment they lost their human life and even though vampires could be destroyed, they were already damned, so it wasn't like bloodlust would be the one thing keeping them from going to heaven or anything like that. In another journal, there was a different point of view, which related the soul to humanity in a different way. As long as the vampire could still feel compassion, love… the soul was still there, even if it wasn't whole.

I was afraid that Matt was far too gone from those feelings, but I had to find a way to cure Matt. There had to be a way of him controlling what he was becoming… or reverse what he had already become.

I glanced at my watch and realized that it was probably already getting dark outside. I knew I had been here for hours, but I completely forgot that I had left the shower on. I rushed out of the room, jumped in the shower for a few minutes, then wrapped a towel around me and walked into my room.

Nicholas was sitting on my bed. He looked me up and down. "Why does Anne have to have so many rules?" He said, as he smiled.

That made me uncomfortable, and he noticed it.

"I'm just kidding, Lexi. By the way, I know I haven't been human for centuries, but is it normal for humans to be in showers for that long?"

I looked at him startled. I had really messed up. "How long have you been in here?!"

He shrugged. "I don't know, about thirty minutes."

"Well, yeah, I guess it can be normal, besides I lost track of time. Now do you mind?" I looked at the door. "I gotta get dressed."

"Oh, come on! Are you sure I can't stay?" He smiled again, only this time I knew he was just messing with me.

"Out!"

Nicholas put his hands up, as in a sign that he was giving up on tormenting me "Alright, alright," and he left.

* * *

When I went downstairs, they were all just hanging out in the living room. That had to be the weirdest thing, vampires just hanging around doing normal things. Lars, Nicholas, and Matt, all playing a video game. Anne was just sitting on the couch reading one of those gossip magazines.

Not one of them looked at me as I made my way into the kitchen. Great, not only am I seen as the human, as Nicholas' pet, but now I'm invisible on top of that. I made my way into the kitchen, I wasn't really hungry so I just grabbed a cereal bar and went to sit on the recliner, which was the farthest away from everyone.

The doorbell rang, and I was really starting to hate that sound. My stomach clenched. Someone at the door in this house was never a good thing.

Anne dropped her magazine and rushed to the door.

"Hi Anne, I got your message that you have something for me. I came right away!"

Even the girl's voice annoyed me.

She came in following Anne, like a little puppy. I had never seen her around before. The girl was tanned, clearly not a vampire. She was tall, thin, but not too skinny, long black hair, green eyes, … she was actually really pretty. Lars, Nicholas, and even Matt, all stopped playing the game and came to welcome her.

Anne ignored Lars and Nicholas and introduced the girl, Denise, to Matt.

"Matt, she is here to pick up that bag of clothes that I showed you earlier, would you mind taking her upstairs and showing it to her?"

"Not at all," he smiled at the girl, which felt like a knife's twist in my stomach.

I just sat there as everyone went back to do what they were doing.

A few minutes later, I took my untouched cereal bar back into the kitchen, threw it in the trash and went upstairs.

I walked past Anne's door, which was closed, and as I approached my room, I realized that my door was open. I don't remember leaving it open.

I approached my room slowly, and when I got to the door and saw what was happening inside my room, I stood there, frozen, unable to move.

The girl, Denise, lay lifeless on my bed; Matt held her wrist to his mouth, as he drank her blood. The girl had lost a lot of color; I knew she was dead. I stood there for a few seconds, before Matt realized that I was there.

Tears rolling down my cheeks, I felt cold, terrified and hurt; yet, I couldn't look away, or even run away.

Matt met my gaze and instantly dropped the girl's wrist.

"Lex, I didn't mean to..."

I thought I heard and saw a glimpse of the old Matt in there, but that was not enough. I ran across the hall into Nicholas' room, which was luckily unlocked and closed the door, hoping that Matt would not follow me.

Chapter 16

At first, I frantically looked around for a place to hide, but once a few minutes passed and no one had tried to come in, I didn't see the need to hide anymore. I figured that if Matt followed me, he must have stopped at the door.

I quickly took another look around, taking in everything about Nicholas' room, just in case I did end up having to hide. His room actually looked like a normal room. The walls were dark gray, which made the room look even darker. He had a couple of paintings on the wall, which looked like they were from centuries back, a huge plasma TV, a couple of dressers and a bed. He actually had a bed! And then there was a mini-fridge right next to the bed, which I knew without a doubt that it would be a bad idea to look inside it.

I took a step away from the door and my legs felt numb. I was shaking and in complete shock of what I had just seen Matt do.

I lay down on Nicholas' bed, put a pillow over my head and started sobbing.

I didn't even hear anyone coming in, but I felt someone sitting on the bed next to me, moving the pillow away and asking if I needed anything.

I was surprised that Nicholas stayed even after seeing that I had been crying; he hated that. I didn't respond when he asked if I was okay and I was surprised he didn't just kick me out of his room.

"I guess, just…you know, call me if you need anything," he said, in a tone that I couldn't determine if it was concern, sympathy, or just being nice so that I would hurry up and leave his room.

Still sobbing, I nodded.

Nicholas simply walked out, locking the door behind him.

* * *

I spent that night and the following day in Nicholas' room, mostly sleeping, on and off. It was already almost dawn on Monday when Nicholas woke me up. I didn't even know how I had been able to fall asleep, but somehow I did.

"You do understand that he cannot control this, right?" He asked.

I nodded, but there was a huge gap between understanding something and actually accepting it.

I got up and I felt nothing but anger. "Is he out of my room?" I asked Nicholas.

Nicholas nodded and I left his room and started going back to mine. When I walked inside of my room, it was all the same as it had been before I had found Matt and that girl in there. No sign of blood; yet, I just kept staring at the bed, my bed, where not too long ago, there was a dead girl lying on it.

Nicholas walked behind me. "You stay in my room until day time. I will have a new bed ordered for your room."

I looked at him, nodded a thanks and left.

I didn't go back to his room. I went down the stairs where I found Matt and Anne sitting side by side on the couch. I walked past them without so much as glancing in their direction, grabbed the keys and left the house.

I drove around for hours, trying unsuccessfully not to think about anything. I wondered how long until Tyler finished whatever it was that Anne wanted him, Loren and Adrianne to do; wondering how long until he would return so that we could just leave.

I kept thinking about all of the times when I asked Tyler to turn me, and he wouldn't because he said I would change, and as much as I hated to admit it, he was right. After all, Matt changed, he wasn't the same anymore, and that could happen to me… But mostly, I wondered if there was a way to save Matt.

* * *

I went back to the house and dropped the car off so that they could ride to school. I walked.

At school, Nicholas mostly kept to himself, almost as if he sensed that I needed space. Truthfully, he had eased up a lot on following me around everywhere.

All of my classes were pretty much the same. I just doodled in my notebooks, ignoring everything and everyone.

"I'm taking you home," Nicholas said.

We still had two classes left, but I didn't care. When that class was over we just left. I was sure Nicholas had taken care of our excuses to leave.

Nicholas stopped the car in the driveway, but didn't shut off the engine.

I looked at him, without saying anything.

"I have to go back for Anne and Lars. Just call me if you need anything."

I nodded and went inside.

In my room, I found a brand new bed. No signs of the bed that I had since I was a kid. I realized that what was upsetting me so much was not what Matt had done to that girl, but what he had done to her, on my bed.

I dropped my books and handbag in my room and went into the secret room where I spent the rest of the day. Not reading about vampires, but mostly just sleeping, trying to see if Tyler could somehow contact me through my dreams, which once again didn't happen. I was more tempted than ever to just call Tyler back to me. He had said he would find a way to get to me, but I didn't want to risk his safety for my selfish reasons, so I decided against it.

* * *

It was about dinnertime when I walked out of the secret room into the bathroom and then into my room.

Matt stood at the door.

"Hi, Lex. Can I come in?" He looked down as if he expected me to say no, but something about the way he asked me made my heart melt.

"Sure," I said, hoping that I would not regret my words. Hoping that Nicholas would be close enough to hear me if I needed help.

Matt seemed to be okay, he didn't look hungry, I could tell by looking in his eyes, and he actually looked sorry for what had happened the other night.

He came in, but stood on the other side of the room, across from me.

"What is the deal with you and that guy?" He looked hurt.

Okay. That I didn't expect.

"You mean, Tyler?"

He nodded.

Some of that pain in his eyes turned into anger. "Scarlett showed me…well, I know everything that happened between you and him…"

"Matt, I didn't." I paused, looking down. I couldn't meet his gaze. "I didn't think I would ever see you again."

"Yeah, I get that, but if I were in your place, I don't think I would have moved on that quickly."

That irritated me. "Oh, and what exactly was that with that girl, Denise, besides you don't care about me anymore. You changed."

He gave me a sarcastic laugh. "That girl was only dinner…and I'm not the only one who changed!"

His words were hurting me almost more than seeing what he had done to that girl. "Matt, you have no idea what my life was like after that plane crash. I felt like I died with you."

He didn't say anything to that. Matt had his head down, as if avoiding my gaze just as much as I avoided his.

After a long pause, Matt slowly lifted his head up. His eyes were darker; and whenever his eyes were either darker or glowing red, it meant that he was thirsty. I took a few steps back, until I felt my back against the wall. Matt got closer to me so fast. He had his hands against the wall, one on each side of me, right above my shoulders, and I had no way out.

I couldn't scream. I couldn't move…and I was pretty sure that if no one heard us arguing and came into my room, was because no one was home. I just stood there, closed my eyes, and waited for the worst.

I felt his body getting closer to me, I got colder, and then I felt his lips on mine. I felt relief and comfort…. kissing Matt felt exactly the same as it did when he was human.

Tyler.

I pushed Matt away, and I was surprised by my own strength.

Matt snarled, exposed his fangs and in a blur, moved back in my direction, pressing me against the wall with his body. He was getting ready to bite me when he pulled away and dropped to the floor.

It was the necklace. It worked!

"Lex…" he sounded weak, but I knew he would recover and he would recover quickly so I needed to act fast.

I ran out of my room. I went downstairs, and then out of the house.

Everyone was gone, like I thought they were, but they had left the car, so I got in and drove away, my heart still racing.

I didn't drive far. I found an empty parking lot, shut off the engine, closed my eyes and laid my head against the back of the seat, trying to figure out what I needed to do.

I couldn't tell Nicholas what had happened, he would tell Anne and she would hurt Matt. Apparently, I couldn't leave the house, but if I stayed I would be in danger all the time

Who was I kidding? I was in more danger than I had anticipated. I didn't know if the necklace would protect me at all times, I mean…it was just a necklace.

I finally convinced myself that there was only one option left, and I didn't like the risks that Tyler would be taking for me, but I couldn't think of anything else but to call him to me.

That was it, I would drive home, wait until I was sure that the others were back so that I wouldn't be alone with Matt. I would go into the secret room, where I could feel safe and focus, and call Tyler back to me.

Just the thought of having him around again made me feel better.

Chapter 17

Anne

Anne got back to the house late at night; accompanied by some guy she had just met. He looked older, in his late thirties, medium built. He was drunk and he was all over her. When she got to the house, Matt was still weak, but not nearly as weak as before, and he was thirsty...very thirsty.

Anne looked at Matt, rolled her eyes and said. "Well, I was hoping to have a little fun with this one, but you look like you need him more than I do...you can have him."

By that time, the guy was already passed out drunk on the couch. Matt looked at him funny.

Anne snarled. "Blood is blood, you can't just feed on girls for the rest of your existence, besides this one looks like he could make you stronger. Just take him upstairs and feed...and don't forget to clean up your mess afterwards."

Matt didn't like it, but he did as he was told.

Shortly after Matt took his meal upstairs, Anne heard a sound coming from outside and went to open the door.

Scarlett stood there; she didn't even say hello.

"Where is Matthew?" Scarlett demanded.

Anne just stared at her.

"He needs me Anne, I can feel he is weak."

Anne motioned for Scarlett to come in the house, and led her to the room where she had previously met with Loren, where she once again was able to relax, letting out her dark wings.

"Matthew's weakness has been taken care of," Anne snapped. Anne actually knew he was weak, but she just didn't care to ask him why.

"Anne!" Scarlett snarled. "I told you from the beginning that Matthew is mine. You asked to have him for a while so he could assist with your little games, but your time is up. I want him back."

"Do not threaten me, Scarlett! You owe me the time I requested, and I will use your boy toy for as long as I see fit... As I recall, you had no business turning the boy to start with. I caused that plane crash because him dying was part of my plan. You and your stupid desperation to have a mate crossed my plan and you are lucky that I allowed you to have him."

Scarlett laughed.

"Do not talk to me like I'm one of your minions! Yes, you are stronger than so many of us, but you seem to often forget just how old I am. We both know that I'm just as strong...and for the record, I owe you nothing."

Anne grinned. "Very well, you are indeed correct Scarlett, and I wouldn't want a simple disagreement getting in the way of our friendship."

Scarlett nodded.

Anne looked as if she was deep in thought. "There might be a way that you could in fact help me achieve my goal faster, should you be willing to."

Scarlett seemed annoyed. "Once again, I do not owe you anything, but go on."

"Why don't you stay with us for the remainder of the evening? Just stay and ensure that Matt is happy and satisfied, especially in front of the human girl. I believe she should return

soon, and I'm sure you would enjoy showing her who Matt really belongs to."

Scarlett grinned. "I believe I will be willing to do that."

"And also, I do not foresee I will need Matt's services any longer, but I would appreciate if I could keep him here just for a few more days."

Scarlett hesitated.

"You will be compensated, Scarlett. Just name your price."

Scarlett always loved making deals in which she would benefit from, especially if she could name her own price. She smiled. "I'm sure I can think of something that I want. Now take me to Matthew."

Chapter 18

Sitting inside the car, at that dark and empty parking lot wasn't going to do me any good. I figured that the sooner I got to the house, the sooner I would be able to get into the secret room and call Tyler back to me.

I was just about to start the car and go home when I saw someone coming in my direction. He looked vaguely familiar. He looked about my age, probably someone I had seen at school. I got the window down just enough to where I could hear him.

"Everything okay over there?" He yelled from the other side of the parking lot.

"Yeah. I was just about to head home."

He started walking faster.

He had a really strong country accent. "Hold up. You are Alexis, right?"

He was standing right by the car now.

I looked up at him with an apologetic expression. "Yeah… I'm sorry, I'm really bad with names… you are?"

"Travis… I'm in your English Lit class."

"Right! Sorry, it is kinda dark outside, I didn't recognize you at first."

I had seen Travis at school a couple of times, he had moved up here from Texas not long ago. He pretty much kept to himself.

I took a good look at him and saw that he was wearing his usual jeans, white t-shirt, and I couldn't see from the inside of the car but I could pretty much guess that he was wearing flip flops, which was better than those cowboy boots that he used to wear all the time. Yeah, not hanging out with anyone besides Nicholas gave me plenty of time to notice details about everyone else, wishing they knew how lucky they all were to have a normal life.

I did think it was strange for him to be just walking around in a dark parking lot.

"So, what are you doing here this late?" I asked him. Ugh, I really need to get home.

"I work over there," he pointed at the store, which I now realized was a pet store. "One of our pets was sick earlier, she wasn't really eating and the boss is out of town so I came over to check on her."

"Oh. That is…sweet," I said awkwardly.

I realized that it had been a while since I last held a face-to-face conversation about normal day-to-day stuff, with someone who didn't see me as a meal.

He must have noticed my expression. "You don't look too good. Are you sure you are alright?"

"Yeah, I'm good. Just roommate problems, I guess… just needed a break."

He grinned. "Well, that is understandable. No offense, but your roommates are kinda creepy."

That made me laugh.

"Hey, why don't you come in the store for a little while. I got to check on the dog again and close everything up. I could use some help."

I couldn't say no to that, not when he was asking so nicely, and nice was something that I didn't get much of lately. I definitely needed a break…normal stuff at least for a little while.

Travis had that southern gentleman thing going on. Once I agreed to help him, which was almost instantly, he opened the car door for me and closed it once I was out.

"So, why do you think my roommates are creepy?" I couldn't help but to ask.

He shrugged. "Between you and me, it is kinda like they are in a cult or something. You know, the way they keep to themselves, not involved in any school activities, and they seem kinda overprotective of you."

He definitely wasn't too far off. I smiled, hoping he didn't notice how nervous I was. "Nah, it is really not what it seems... and they are not that bad." The last thing I needed was to have to worry about putting him in danger. I tried to come up with a lame excuse for the overprotective comment.

"They just feel responsible for me in a way...you know, because my parents allow me to live in their house and all."

Luckily, he left it at that. We walked into the store and there was a pizza box sitting on the counter and it smelled great. Even that amused me... at the house I couldn't just leave stuff like that lying around because no one could stand the smell of it. I was surprised they didn't just put a fridge and microwave inside my room, so they wouldn't have to look at it either.

Travis saw me staring at the box.

"You are welcome to have some."

"Oh, no, I'm fine..."

He smiled. "Come on. Coach Carson will get on me if I eat that whole thing anyways."

Coach Carson was the school's swim team coach.

"You are on the swim team?" Okay, that was a stupid question.

"Yep"

To avoid an awkward silence, I gave in and grabbed a slice of pepperoni pizza and then followed Travis to the back of the store.

When we got to the store's office, the cutest little golden retriever puppy came running to Travis.

He picked her up, petting her head.

"Guess she feels better."

The puppy looked at me, basically begging for the pizza, but I remembered Travis saying that she was sick, so I hurried to finish eating.

"You let them just run around in the store?" Talk about being dedicated to a job.

"Yeah…well, one at a time," he smiled. "They take turns… wanna hold her?"

"Sure!" I took the last bite and took the golden retriever from Travis' hands.

"What is her name?"

"Well, we are not supposed to name them…store policy, but I tend to ignore a lot of those…so, her name is Gracey," he said, while petting her.

"You really like pets, huh?"

"Yeah, they are good company. No drama, no complications." Wow, he was right about that.

There was an awkward silence for a couple of minutes, while we just stood there, petting Gracey.

"So, how is it living with roommates? No parents?" He asked.

I shrugged. "It is not all that great."

Talking about my roommates brought me back to reality. I looked at my watch and it was well past eleven.

"I really need to get going."

"Alright. Let me just get everything ready and I will walk out with you. It won't take long."

Travis took Gracey and put her back in her kennel. He grabbed the pizza box and threw it away, after I declined the offer of taking the rest of it home. He then turned the lights off, and we walked out door and he locked up the store.

As he walked me to the car, I looked around the parking lot. "I don't see your car, do you need a ride?"

He shook his head. "Nah, I parked behind the store."

"Aw, you didn't have to walk me all the way here if your car is the other way."

He smiled. "Yeah, I did."

He opened the car door for me and I thanked him for everything.

"No problem. You know, if you ever want to get away from your roommates long enough to hang out you should just come over here, or even if you want a change of pace at school and hang out with someone different… I really don't know a lot of people in town yet, my boyfriend lives in Texas…" Did he just say boyfriend? He noticed I looked surprised. "Yeah... boyfriend. Probably the reason the guys in the swim team really limit the time they spend with me, but whatever. I'm not really one to hide secrets. I'm an open book!" I wish I could say the same.

"We will definitely hang out, Travis... and as for the swim team...it is their loss."

I smiled thinking how nice would be to have a good friend, a good human friend.

I gave him a hug. Hoping that Nicholas would at least back off a little at school so that I could hang out with Travis without him hovering and without putting Travis in danger.

I got in the car and drove off feeling rejuvenated and wishing life was always this simple and normal.

Chapter 19

I opened the door to the house and immediately saw her sitting on the couch next to Matt, way too close for comfort. And seeing Matt with her wrist on his mouth, sucking her blood while she kissed his neck just drove me over the edge. The feeling of being rejuvenated didn't last long. I was so exhausted...tired to the point where my judgment was impacted and I acted on impulse.

"You bitch!" I shouted as I walked in her direction. I didn't care who or what she was, I didn't even know what exactly I was going to do once I reached her, all I knew was that I wanted her away from Matt, but I was stopped before I could get to her.

The woman let go of Matt's neck, which I now saw that she wasn't just kissing, but she was drinking from him as well. She slowly pulled her wrist away from his mouth, and then she looked at me and gave a sarcastic grin.

Lars held me back with much more strength than needed. He had his arm wrapped around me and I as much as I tried to get away; I was completely unable to move.

"You are hurting me!" I yelped.

He didn't let go at all. The necklace wasn't working. I hoped that was because Lars wasn't really planning on hurting me, even if by him holding me back was going to leave bruises on my arm. After a while, I gave up trying get away, that was only making me more tired and no matter how much I tried to move around, Lars didn't move an inch.

I glanced at Matt hoping that he would help me break free, but he looked dazed. I knew none of this was his fault. His soul, humanity, or whatever he is missing has to be in there somewhere. I have to find a way to help him, which means I can't call Tyler back to me just yet.

The woman met my gaze, still smiling.

In any other circumstances, this woman would have looked harmless, she looked fragile, light skin, small frame, long wavy brown hair, her eyes were darker than most of them, but it wasn't the same darkness as from when they were hungry.

She just looked completely harmless; except for the way she talked and carried herself.

"I assume you are Alexis… Hello, I'm Scarlett."

Now I knew why I felt so repulsed by her, Scarlett was Matt's maker, the one who turned him.

I stared at her, not saying anything, doing my best not to look away; not to show any sign of weakness.

"Hmm… you are not quite what I expected," Scarlett said.

She turned to face Anne who I just now realized stood by the door, looking as if she was entertained by all of this. I looked around and Nicholas was nowhere in sight.

Scarlett got up, still facing Anne.

"Anne, Matthew may stay as long as necessary. I believe I know what I want in return."

She paused, looked at Matt, and the mere sound of her voice was enough to get his attention right away.

"My dear, I must go now, but it won't be long until you are able to come back home to me."

For a second, I even forgot that Lars was holding me back; I just stood there, motionless. And then I saw Matt standing up. He turned to face Scarlett and kissed her! The kiss was intense enough to make me look away. To keep the tears from coming I kept telling myself he doesn't want this, none of this is his fault or his choice. And even though I was officially with Tyler, watching Matt with Scarlett was still painful.

I was only aware that they had stopped kissing because she walked by me, and stopping as if she was taking in my scent, she made a sound as if she just smelled the thing that she craved the most, which sent shivers through my entire body, making the hair on my arm stand up. I just looked away, that was all I could do. Lars still held me back so I was unable to move and I had now enough common sense not to speak to her, even though I was calling her all sorts of names in my head.

Scarlett kept moving towards the door.

"Anne, you will hear from me soon with my request," and she walked out.

The door closed behind her and this time, when I glanced at Matt, there was something different in his eyes. Regret? Pain? Whatever it was, it gave me hope that I could bring him back from this darkness that he was trapped within, but right now, I could barely even look at him.

In almost a whisper, he said, "Lex, I..."

I cut him off and turned my head as much as I could in Lars' direction and snapped, "Let go of me!"

Lars let go without saying a word. Ugh. I really couldn't stand him.

I stormed out of the living room without so much as looking at any of them, including Matt who I heard whisper my name once again, as I walked past him.

Chapter 20

In the morning it all seemed like nothing had happened. Matt was not around, because, well… it was daytime, and unlike the others, daylight would probably destroy him, sunlight, definitively would.

Lars, Anne and Nicholas, were all ready to go to school when I got downstairs. No one said anything about the night before, including me. I wasn't even sure if Nicholas knew what happened, but I assumed that he did, considering that he was staring at the bruises on my arm; bruises caused by Lars holding me back the night before. But even after noticing the bruises, Nicholas didn't ask anything about it.

Fortunately that did remind me that the bruises were there, so I put on my Gap hoodie and followed them outside.

The ride to school was quiet.

Once we got to school, Lars and Anne went their own way, and Nicholas and I headed to our first class of the day.

"Sooo, I hear you met Scarlett last night," he said with a grin.

I was already in a horrible mood before I even heard her name.

"Yeah, I did meet her and I'm not talking about it."

I started walking faster, getting ahead of him, not that I would be able to get away, because he was in all of my classes.

I was tired, mostly from lack of sleep, and I assumed that Nicholas likely knew that Scarlett was coming before it even happened, so I got mad at him for not being there, after all, he was the only one who had the guts to stand up to Anne and Lars.

He caught up with me. "You know, even if I was there, I would have been outnumbered."

I ignored him and kept walking.

* * *

I spent most of my two first classes doodling on my notebook. After that I went to my third period class, English Lit. That was one of the few classes where we did not have assigned seats. I got in, and saw Travis. He waved at me and pointed to the one empty seat next to him. I looked back at Nicholas, who for the first time looked surprised.

I didn't even think much about the consequences of Nicholas knowing that I somehow found time away to meet a new friend, or if that would put Travis in any danger. I simply turned my back to Nicholas and went to sit by Travis.

Travis turned out to be the cure for my horrible mood. He got my phone number in the beginning of the class, and through out the entire class, we texted each other back and forth. Travis was mostly playing a game of what not to wear as he commented on pretty much everyone's outfits.

Every once in a while I saw Nicholas looking back, still confused, but I just ignored his gaze.

After that class, we all went to lunch. Well, I went with Travis, Nicholas walked in front of us, meeting Anne and Lars, who instantly saw me with Travis, and looked just as confused as Nicholas.

After we sat down, Travis noticed that we were being watched.

"See, told ya…they are like a cult or something weird like that."

I shrugged, no longer making any effort to disagree.

I tried to find a way to change topics, and started working on an excuse to get out of the house that afternoon.

"So, do you need help at the pet store today?"

"Well, I don't work today, but I might still stop by and check on things…boss is still out of town. Wanna come?"

"Yeah," I smiled.

Then we went on to talk about his boyfriend who still lived in Texas, and how the long distance relationship thing wasn't working out too well for them.

Lunch was over in no time, and I agreed to meet Travis after school and ride with him to the store.

During my next class, I was going to be sitting by Nicholas, but at least I was in a better mood, and no longer felt the need to take anything out on Nicholas. Poor guy, truthfully, none of what happened the night before was his fault.

I sat down and he just shook his head.

"Lars said your new friend smells good," he said, as if that was part of a normal conversation to have.

I lowered my voice so no one could hear me, and in an annoyed tone said, "You tell Lars that if he so much as touches Travis, I will tell Anne that he broke her house rule and drank blood from me."

Nicholas looked at me startled, but not in a bad way. "Wow! I guess you have been spending too much time around us…getting brave. I would actually love to see all of that play out."

"Whatever. Just tell him that."

"You have more than Lars to worry about. Just know that

I will not get in the middle of this, I have other priorities, and you are in no way to expect me to protect your little friend."

I turned and faced the front of the classroom, not thinking of anything but a way to protect Travis from all of this.

I could give him the locket necklace. Like he was gonna wear that… not really a guy necklace. Well, it wasn't really about the necklace so much as the symbol, maybe I could go out in town and get something that he would wear and have the symbol engraved on it. That is it! I felt much better now. Sometime during the day I would just ask Travis to take me to a store, although he would probably think I was weird for getting him something like that, but I didn't have any other ideas.

* * *

When my last class of the day was over, I walked out with Nicholas. I wasn't even sure what kind of car Travis drove, so, I just walked towards the general direction I usually did. I was just getting my phone out to text Travis and find out where he was, when I heard the sound of his horn, I turned around to see Travis driving an RX8, which was totally weird. Texas guy…country accent…cowboy boots…I half expected him to be driving a pick-up truck.

I turned to face Nicholas, and Lars and Anne were right behind him.

"I got a couple things to do. I will see you all later." That was all I said.

I got into Travis' car and he drove off.

Travis laughed. "Are you really sure there is nothing weird going on with them?"

"Yeah, pretty sure...I guess," I grinned.

"Hey, I hope you don't mind, but I have a swim thing at school in about an hour. I totally forgot about it.... If you don't want to come I can just drop you off first."

"No, I'm good...nothing else to do."

"Oh, that makes me feel good about myself... I'm your last resort plan," he laughed.

I rolled my eyes. "It is not like that."

"Yeah, I know, just messing with you."

We went out to the pet store, then back to the school. Travis actually had a regular swim practice. He had made it sound like something important when he said he had a swim thing, but I guess he just didn't want to ditch.

After what I had heard about the swim team guys being a jerk to Travis, I thought it was better to just stay away; I knew it wouldn't take much to put me in a bad mood again. So, I just read a book, while Travis practiced.

When it was all over and he came out of the locker room, he was wearing jeans, flip flops and no shirt. Let's just say that his boyfriend was a lucky guy.

Apparently Travis got his shirt wet, but he had another one in the car. When he turned around to walk to his car, I saw the small, black tattoo on his back, between his shoulder blades. Once I focused on what I was looking at, I realized that his tattoo was the same exact symbol that was on my locket necklace, the five-pointed star that symbolized protection.

"Hey, when did you get that?" I asked him.

"Oh, the tattoo?" He laughed. "Sometimes I even forget

it is there. I got it a couple of years back. Kind of a family tradition."

"Oh."

"Yeah, it is silly, but it is sorta cool that everyone in the family has it."

"What does it mean?" I asked wondering if he knew of its true meaning. It was all too much of a coincidence.

"From what I heard it is for protection. My mom always made fun of this tradition.... She always says 'only the Crowel's would need silly protection against the boogeyman'... She doesn't like the whole tattoo idea, especially when you are under eighteen."

I was glad that he was protected, that was one less thing in my mind, but I froze in place as I heard his last name. "Did you just say your last name is Crowel?"

"Yep."

"Did you know there were others with the same last name in the school... in fact, my boyfriend...Tyler Crowel."

"I heard, but we are probably not even related at all. That is quite a common last name, besides, all my family is from the south.... but anyways, I never met them, they were actually gone when I got here...so, you still date him?"

"Yeah."

"I guess we got the long distance relationship fiasco in common."

"We sure do. Although you probably get to talk to your boyfriend more often than I do."

He shrugged. "One way or another, long distance sucks."

On the ride home I started to wonder if he was related to Loren, I knew that Tyler and Adrianne weren't actually born Crowel's, but Loren was. What was I gonna say… Oh, do you by any chance have an ancestor whose name was Loren? Right!

Chapter 21

I couldn't hide from my problems forever. I sat in my room thinking about what Scarlett said to Anne, about allowing Matt to stay longer. It was clear that Anne liked drama… playing mind games for some reason was her favorite pastime, and whatever grudge Anne had with me, it was obvious that she figured out that my weakness was Matt.

It annoyed me that I didn't know what her fascination was in playing these games with me, out of all humans, but in a way, I was glad that her requesting Matt to stay longer would allow me more time to save his humanity, whatever of it there was to be saved.

* * *

For the next few days, things calmed down, mostly because I spent the days hanging out with Travis. Nicholas and the others backed off a little and Travis even got me a part time job at the pet store where he worked.

At nights, I would lock myself in my room avoiding everyone, as I focused on reading the journals out of the secret room. I read them back-to-back, trying unsuccessfully to find anything that I could use to help Matt.

Well, I did actually find something that could help Matt, but in a different way. I had heard about this before, but it was one of those things that I just never considered as an actual option, so I didn't think much about it.

I learned that what vampires needed in order to be able to go out into daylight and even sunlight, was to have the blood of mixed breeds within their system. A few centuries back, when that was first discovered, vampires were having children with humans just to be able to drink from their offspring, which allowed them to go out in daylight; only that started to increase their risk of exposure and eventually became forbidden by whoever enforced their rules. Now, the only way to be able to go out into daylight was to drink from a vampire who could; a vampire who carried that mixed blood in their system… the problem was that they didn't want to give more vampires that power. This ability turned out to be an advantage over others. My only option would probably have been to ask Adrianne or maybe even Loren to allow Matt to drink their blood, but I knew that Matt was too much of a risk…they wouldn't even consider it.

For that time being, I had to just put aside everything that I had learned. It was exhausting that whenever I found out anything like that; I had to push it out of my mind so that Nicholas and the others couldn't sense exactly how much I knew.

* * *

That night, when I stepped out of the secret room, into the bathroom, and then into my bedroom, my heart skipped a beat, as I saw Matt in my room. He was sitting on my bed, motionless; his head was down.

"Matt?"

He slowly lifted his head and his eyes were blood shot, bloody tears ran down his cheeks. He wiped them with the back of his hand.

I wanted to approach him. I hesitated at first, but then I remembered that I was wearing the necklace, I knew I would be fine.

I sat on the bed next to Matt.

"Are you okay?" I asked even though I knew that clearly he was far from being okay.

He didn't say anything at first. He put his hand on mine and out of reflex I pulled my hand away. I didn't pull my hand away because I was afraid of him, his touch just felt odd. Matt used to be one of those people who no matter how cold it was, he was always warm.

The pain in his eyes from me pulling my hand away from him, made me feel horrible. This was as close to the real Matt as I got since he came to this house, and now I was pushing him away from me.

I put my hand on his.

He met my gaze, and his eyes were no longer as red as they were when he was crying.

"Lex, I'm so sorry. I only came here to find you, to be with you. All I wanted was to try and get you back…I didn't mean for any of the other stuff to –"

He stopped mid sentence. I felt his hands getting colder."

"I know you didn't mean for anything to happen, Matt."

Just like that, Matt wasn't there anymore. His eyes went completely dark with hunger and desire, but his transformation into this dark guy who sat by my side didn't matter. I had let my guard down, and I was lost in the sound of his voice.

Unfortunately, the necklace only protected me from direct physical attacks…

I felt light-headed at first. Matt approached me, putting his arms around my waist, pulling me closer, and he kissed me…long…sweet…intense, and I was completely under his control. I knew what was happening, I just had no will to fight it, to fight him.

Matt lured me into taking the necklace off. He wouldn't be able to take it off himself; once the necklace was on, only I could take it off, and I did. I didn't even hesitate.

In a zombie-like motion, I removed the necklace, then

stood up and walked to my dresser where I put it in my jewelry box.

"The other one too, Lex," he said in a sweet voice, referring to the other necklace that I wore, the one that belonged to Tyler's ancestors, a family jewel, that Tyler's mom gave to me and Tyler insisted that I kept.

Glamoured, dazed, I took that necklace off and put it with the gold locket necklace in my jewelry box.

When I turned around, Matt was standing in front of me.

"Lex, you know that I'm only doing this because I want us to be together, right?"

I nodded.

I felt Matt's cold fingers as he brushed my hair off my face, then moved my hair to the side as he tilted my head, leaving my neck exposed. I felt his cold lips as he started to kiss my neck, and then he just stopped.

I straightened my neck, and glanced at him. He was staring at a picture on my dresser. It was a homecoming picture taken in Florida on our sophomore year in high school. In this picture, there was my friend Leah, who had made homecoming court. Leah was no longer with us. After we went to Italy a few months back, she had met someone, Josh. He got turned into a vampire and tried to turn her, only his maker got involved, and it all went horribly wrong…and I lost my best friend.

In that picture, there was also Leah's date for the dance, whose name I couldn't remember, and then there was Matt, when he was still human, and me… things were so much simpler back then.

After a few minutes, Matt broke his focus away from the

picture and stared at me.

His eyes were still dark, but he sounded different, more in control of his actions, more careful.

"Lex, you need to get away from me as fast you can. Do you understand?"

I nodded.

Whatever spell he had me under faded immediately. I was confused, and shaking, but his last words were all I could think of… get away from me…fast… On instinct, I grabbed both of the necklaces out of the jewelry box and ran.

Within seconds I could hear the sound of Matt's footsteps. As he followed me, I knew he was fast and I would never outrun him, but without so much as looking back, I kept running as fast as I could.

Chapter 22

It didn't take but a few seconds before Matt stopped me. I had been running down the stairs when he grabbed my shoulder and turned me around with such force that my back slammed against the wall, and the necklaces that I was holding, which included the one that was supposed to protect me, just flew out of my hand.

My whole body ached and I felt dizzy, disoriented, probably because of the impact from being basically thrown against the wall. I could have screamed, but that would not have done me any good. It was clear that Matt and I were the only ones in the house, and Matt was well aware of that as well.

This time, Matt didn't waste time and there was nothing that I could have done to stop him, not without that necklace, not with this "version" of Matt standing in front of me.

His eyes were dark, empty and cold. He pulled me away from the wall, and closer to him. My entire body felt limp and I would probably just have fallen on the stairs if it wasn't for Matt having his arm around my waist, holding me up. Matt used his other hand to move my hair out of his way as he approached my neck.

I tried to fight him but I could barely move.

My voice sounded weak and shaken. "Matt, don't do this! Not this way..."

He didn't even so much as hesitate, or say anything. I felt his cold lips on my neck, the sharp cut as his fangs punctured through my skin, and I could smell the blood, my blood.

I knew when he started to actually drink my blood because of the moaning sound he made as he pulled me closer to him and at that exact same time, I started to feel as if I was paralyzed. Even if he allowed me to, I couldn't move; I couldn't scream. I knew that was when the venom had been released into my system.

It was painful, but not as unbearable as knowing that Matt was doing this. He stood there, seeing what was happening to me, yet, he wouldn't stop drinking my blood.

Within minutes my breathing started to slow down and I started getting colder, the venom was starting to spread through my body.

I saw something moving so fast towards Matt that it looked more like a shadow. It wasn't until it got closer that I realized that the shadow wasn't really a shadow; it was Nicholas and Lars.

Nicholas snarled. "Let her go!"

I could feel Matt retracting his fangs as they slowly ripped out of my skin. Nicholas pulled me out of Matt's arms, and into his, as Lars dragged Matt down the stairs and to the other side of the room, holding Matt by his neck.

Nicholas scooped me up into his arms and rushed me to the couch.

I felt cold and weak, but I still had enough energy to keep my eyes open. In a useless attempt to keep my mind out of what was happening to me, I tried to use that energy to see what was happening around me.

From the other side of the room, I heard Matt saying my name and after that I couldn't keep my gaze away from him. I watched as he struggled to get away from Lars. Matt looked terrified, as if he had just realized what happened. Then I saw Anne moving towards him with such anger, that I even made an attempt to get up, but I couldn't move at all. I gave one pleading look at Nicholas, who just looked at me as if he was trying to assess the damage.

In an urgent tone, Nicholas stopped Anne before she could get to Matt.

"Anne, I need your help here! NOW!"

Surprisingly, Anne rushed to my side. She glanced at me and then she looked at Nicholas. She seemed furious.

Not once looking away from Nicholas' gaze she said. "Lars, do not let Matthew go. Nicholas, start sucking the venom out when I tell you to."

Nicholas nodded.

Anne held both of my hands in hers. She closed her eyes, and I instantly felt warmer and started gaining my senses back. Then she opened her eyes and looked at Nicholas. "Now!"

Nicholas took his shirt off and wiped my neck with it. He can't seriously be afraid to be getting Matt's germs!"

Nicholas bit me around the same spot as Matt, only now my neck was sore and it hurt that much more. As soon as he bit me, he retracted his fangs to prevent his venom from being released, and he started drinking my blood.

Every second, I felt stronger and I could feel that strength was coming from whatever Anne was doing. After a while, not more than a few minutes, Anne ordered him to stop and as soon as he stopped, Anne let go of my hands.

Anne didn't even ask me if I was okay. She simply moved in Matt's direction, ordering Lars to let go, and she took over his place.

Matt was up against the wall, held back only by Anne's hand around his neck.

I tried to sit up, but Nicholas ordered me to stay.

"You are not strong enough," he looked at Anne, who was staring into Matt's eyes. "Anne, you should take it easy. You lost a lot of energy just now."

She didn't even acknowledge him.

She snarled at Matt. "Was I unclear about what the house rules were?"

His only response was enough to melt my heart; he actually still cared about me. "What do you want with Lex?"

In a warning tone she continued. "Listen to me very carefully. What I do is none of your concern. And you so much as try to cross me again and I will destroy you. I destroyed you once, and I can do it again."

Matt looked as confused as I was. Anne leaned closer to him and whispered something in his ear; something that I would not have been able to hear if it wasn't for the strength I gained from whatever Anne had just done to me.

"Airplanes don't just crash for no reason."

Matt laughed. "Are you trying to say that you caused the crash? The one that killed me?... Right!"

Anne just stared at him, as I tried to process what was happening. I can't possibly be hearing this right. I'm probably still messed up from all of this…

Nicholas glared at Anne.

"Enough with this nonsense, Anne. Lexis' healing took a lot from you. You need to go," he warned her.

"Not until he pays!"

I stood up as fast as I could. Nicholas was surprised, but he kept me from going closer to Anne and Matt.

I met Anne's gaze. "Don't! Let him go… please."

Anne looked puzzled.

"You still care for him, even after what happened?"

I nodded.

"After everything, you still care for him?"

"Yes!"

"Interesting, you are stronger than –" She stopped mid-sentence.

"Stronger than who?"

"It is not important."

I felt stronger, I would never have asked what I did if it wasn't for how different I felt.

"Did you cause Matt's plane crash?"

She let him go and smiled. "Don't be silly, I was just messing with him. Causing a plane crash would not have been physically possible now, would it?"

I started to feel dizzy again. I lost my balance, and Nicholas caught me. Anne still stared at me, looking for an answer.

"I guess not, but…"

"That is enough with the questions. You need rest… I will allow Matt to go, unharmed… and no need to worry about being imprinted with Nicholas, I'm sure you can sense that didn't happen, and you can thank me for that later."

She faced Matt. "Matthew, you are no longer welcome in

this house. Be gone before dawn." She then looked at Nicholas. "Alexis is your responsibility until he leaves."

"What do you want in exchange for Lexi?" Matt asked.

Anne laughed, she sounded and looked cold. "You have nothing that I wish to have."

She turned around, and left, ordering Nicholas and I to go upstairs, where she walked into her room, and Nicholas and I went into his, leaving Matt struggling to get past Lars, not because Matt still wanted to harm me, at least not at this moment. Before we went upstairs, Matt just looked as if he wanted to get me away from Anne, away from this house. But even if he had gotten his way and taken me with him, I would still be in danger, because the Matt who had just almost turned me into a vampire could be back within seconds.

Chapter 23

I had been in Nicholas' room only once before and just like then, his room was dark and cold.

I intended to ask him about Anne, about what she had done to keep us from imprinting and to reverse me turning into a vampire, but that strength that I had felt once Anne held my hands while Nicholas got the venom out of my system, slowly started to fade at the moment she let go. Now, I felt sick... weak and light-headed, probably because of all of the blood I had lost.

To keep myself from passing out, I laid down on Nicholas' bed.

"Could you get me something to drink? I feel like I'm dehydrated or something."

"What do you want?" he asked, sounding indifferent.

I subconsciously glanced at the mini-fridge on the right side of his bed. "Anything."

Nicholas noticed that I had looked at the mini-fridge, smiled and in his sarcastic tone said, "Oh, I seriously doubt that. How about some water?"

I nodded, and then closed my eyes.

Nicholas was back within seconds. Anne had made me his responsibility until Matt was no longer in the house and I was sure that leaving me alone for long was a risk that he was not willing to take. I was also sure that Nicholas mixed something in that water, because I fell asleep right away.

* * *

I found myself at the beach. It was warm and I felt safe. I knew it was a dream because I saw Matt sitting on the sand, the sun shinning on him and he just looked… human. He turned around and stood up when he saw me walking towards him.

He kept one hand behind his back, as if he was hiding something and when I stood only inches away from him, he smiled, slowly moving his hand towards me, he gave me a blue rose.

Back when I still thought Matt was dead, well really dead… non-existent, I had been getting those same blue roses. It turned out that Matt had been the one sending me the roses with Nicholas' help, and later I had come to find out the meaning of a blue rose… unattainable, not being able to have someone, yet, unable to keep that person out of your mind. Just the thought of that was in a way a reassurance that Matt, the one I knew back when he was human, was still within this cold and distant version of him.

In that dream, standing at that beach, he gave me the rose and when I took it, he slowly took my hand in his. He brought my hand to his lips, he kissed it, and within seconds, he started to fade away.

I didn't wake up until eleven the next morning. Physically, I felt better, although still a little weak; emotionally, I was scared of how much worse Matt would get, especially now that there was literally nothing that I could do about it.

I had missed school and so had Nicholas, who sat on a chair in his room, watching TV. I didn't care to ask where Anne and Lars were but my guess would be that they were around. They rarely even made it to class anymore.

I managed to sit up on the bed without feeling dizzy.

"Is Matt already gone?" I asked, even though I knew the answer.

Nicholas nodded.

"Do you know where he went?"

Nicholas' gaze didn't leave the TV. "No, and really don't care."

Nicholas stood up, grabbed a paper bag that was on top of the TV stand and handed it to me.

"Here… This is probably not the best meal you need to recover, but…"

"It is fine, thanks." I took the bag from his hand. There must have been at least four different types of biscuits in there. I grabbed a sausage biscuit and started eating it, even though I wasn't hungry.

Nicholas looked amused as he watched me eating.

"What?" I asked him.

"Nothing. I just don't see how humans can eat…you know…food."

In a sarcastic and annoyed tone, I said, "Well, I don't see how vampires can drink blood, so I guess we are even."

Nicholas laughed. "Feeling better, huh?"

I shrugged. " A little."

I stood up and put the bag back on the TV stand.

Nicholas stared at me.

"Don't worry, I will take this out of your room in a few minutes."

I was scared to find out, but I asked him anyways. "How

bad is my neck?"

He pointed at the mirror lying on his dresser. "See if for yourself."

I was really scared to look, my heart raced. When I finally turned the mirror so I could see it, there was nothing on my neck…no bite marks…no scars."

"How—?"

"Anne healed you."

"Is that like her vampire ability?"

"In a way."

That was all I would get out of him. I just loved Nicholas' vague answers.

"Oh," he said as he reached into his pocket and got my cell phone, handing it to me. "This thing has been going off all morning."

I looked at my phone and saw that there were several text messages from Travis, but Nicholas was hovering, so I decided to read them later.

* * *

As soon as I got away from Nicholas' vigilance, my mind was preoccupied with concerns about Matt and how I lost my chance to help him. I should have confronted Anne, I should have told her I would only stay if he did…not that it would have gone well...

I went to the kitchen, grabbed a couple bottles of Gatorade and then went to my room. As soon as I opened the door, I stood there for a few seconds, staring at what was lying on my pillow. A blue rose.

I took a few steps towards my bed. I was barefoot so I instantly felt that there were tracks of sand on my floor. It almost felt as if Matt had stepped out of that dream and into my room. Under the rose, there was a note. I sat on my bed, holding the note in my hands, trembling and not sure if I wanted to read what was in there. As I contemplated reading the note, I looked up at my dresser and saw the empty picture frame. The picture that included Matt and me at homecoming dance when he was still human was gone, but I wasn't upset about it. I was glad that he wanted to take something to remind him of who he really is, or used to be.

That thought gave me the courage to open the note.

Lex,

I now know that you are better off if I stay away from you, but you need to be careful, get out of that house as soon as you can. I'm sorry but I can't trust myself to help you… I'm sorry about everything.

Love you… always,

Matt

"Aw. How romantic!" Anne said in a sarcastic tone. I looked up to see her at the door. "Who would have known that you love him enough that your blood was the key to curing his bloodlust…all that humanity brought back into him."

I avoided her gaze, but she could see that I grinned at the sound of what she had just said.

"Well, don't gloat just yet, darling. He went back to Scarlett, he will be back in the same exact condition probably tonight, when he can get out and hunt again."

I sounded stupid and lame asking her that. "Can't you help him? Stop him from going there?"

"Darling, he is likely already there. Besides, you should accept that this is who he is now. There is no reason in fighting it. Around you, he will always be going back and forth on this helpless battle to keep his humanity...you will just never know when it will be safe."

"But, can't YOU help him?" I asked, wondering if she could heal him somehow.

"It is not a matter of being able to help him, I just won't."

She left before I could say anything else.

I didn't realize that I was crying until a tear dropped on the note that I was still holding.

I got up and closed the door. Still holding the rose in my hand, I laid down and closed my eyes for a while.

I needed to figure out what I should do, I couldn't help Matt anymore. I needed Tyler back with me, but I was afraid of the consequences of me calling him back to me. I was afraid that would put him in bad terms with his maker, Loren. And I was afraid that if I just left, Anne and Lars would go after my parents.

I felt my phone vibrating. It was another text from Travis and I realized that I had forgotten to read all of his previous texts. I went back to the first text he had sent.

"Hey. Where r u 2day? I'm bored as heck!"

Another text... "k...just noticed ur roomies r not here either. Weird! U didn't like join their cult, did u? lol"

And another... "That s it, if u don't reply, I'm coming over after school."

I knew Travis would be able to keep my mind off things,

but with the others in the house that was not such a great idea, even if he had that tattoo to protect him.

I replied. “I’m ok…just been sick.”

He instantly sent another. “k…but I’m coming over anyways.”

Great!

Chapter 24

It didn't matter how many texts I sent Travis asking him not to come over. He had already made up his mind about coming and eventually, I gave in and told him to text me when he was on his way, and that I would be waiting in front of the house.

Giving in seemed to be the theme for the day.

It would be a while before school let out, so I decided it was time to get Tyler back here…with me. There was just no reason for me to stay in this house anymore, or for him to stay away. I was tired of living afraid of the possible consequences of every little action that I took.

I even managed to convince myself that Anne broke her promise to Loren to protect me, and I had the illusion that it would work as a loophole so that I could leave with Tyler without consequences, without putting my parents in danger. Only I wasn't sure if Tyler would know the reason I was calling him to me, or even if Loren would allow him to leave.

I remembered Tyler's words I will find a way to come to you. And that gave me the confidence to do what I needed to do.

Anne and Lars were who-knows-where, and Nicholas was too focused on his video game to notice what I was up to. I walked by him, said I was going to take a nap and went up to my room. Once in my room, I locked the door, went into the bathroom and then into the secret room. I sat in the middle of the room, closed my eyes and focused on Tyler, wishing he were here with me, telling him that I needed him back. As I opened my eyes, I felt better than before, there was something about this room that made me feel relaxed, calm.

I hoped that calling Tyler would get him back here. I grabbed the necklace that he had given me, the one with the angel, held it tight in my hand, wishing I could have a sign that this would work; only there really weren't any signs.

I felt my phone vibrate.

"On my way."

It was Travis. Time had gone by faster than I had anticipated. That happened every time I was in that room.

Minutes later, I met Travis at the door. He had dropped me off at the house once before, so he knew where I lived.

He got out of his car and took a good look at me. "You really should be inside…you know… resting," he said in a concerned tone.

"Yeah, well… I figured that since my roomies creep you out, I'd better answer the door."

"Oh, they are here?" he asked, not sounding too happy about it.

"I think Nicholas may be the only one here… I'm not sure about Anne and Lars."

"Oh." He didn't seem too pleased about seeing any of them.

I personally didn't really want to see Anne or Lars either.

"Hey, do you mind if we hang out at your house instead?"

His face brightened up. "Are you sure you are up for it?"

"Yeah, I feel a lot better…and I really wanted to get away for a few hours."

"Okay," he said cheerfully.

"How about you wait in the car? I will be right out."

I walked back in, Nicholas was still glued to his video

game, so I hoped that he would just nod at whatever I said and I would be on my way out.

I cleared my throat. "Um… I'm going to Travis' house for a while."

"How long is a while?" he asked without looking away from his game.

I shrugged. "I don't know, a few hours, I guess."

Nicholas actually paused the game and put the controller down. He met my gaze and said, "You need to be back before dark or I will be coming to get you myself."

I didn't have to ask him the reason. Crazy how you spend enough time around someone and you start to know how they think. I was sure Nicholas thought that there was a possibility that Matt would come back for me and at night was the only time he would be able to.

I smiled at Nicholas, my best sarcastic smile. "Okay, DAD, I will be home before dark."

"I'm serious, Lexi."

"I know!"

* * *

Travis' house was warm; cozy… it just felt like home, back when I lived with mom and dad.

I could smell the homemade cinnamon muffins that Travis' mom was baking. She came out of the kitchen when she heard us. As soon as she saw me, she smiled. She seemed genuinely happy, there was even a sparkle in her eyes.

She glanced at Travis.

“Son, you should have told me you were bringing someone home. The house is a mess!”

Travis rolled his eyes.

“It was a last minute decision, mom.”

“Well… who is your friend?”

“Hi, Mrs. Crowel. I’m Alexis.”

“Nice to meet you, hon, and please call me Jessica.”

She gave me another warm smile.

“Well, you kids probably have homework to do, and I need to go check on those muffins. I won’t bother you kids, just come on down when you are hungry,” she said, clearly emphasizing that we were going to be hanging out upstairs and unsupervised.

Travis rolled his eyes at his mom once again.

“Come on, Lexi.”

He led me upstairs to his room. We got inside and embarrassed, he said, “Don’t mind my mom. I guess she is still in denial, she has high hopes that I will break up with Rob and start dating girls.” Rob was Travis’ boyfriend, who lived in Texas.

I wasn’t sure what to say. I mean, it must suck that his parents were in denial about who he really was, and that was really too bad. Travis was a great person, and I felt as if I could really trust him.

I finally said, “They will come around.”

He seemed a little sad now, “I doubt it, but anyways…welcome to my room,” he said, as he attempted a smile.

"Nice!" I said as I took a look around.

His walls were blue, and were covered with movie posters, mostly action movies.

"Thanks …so, homework?"

I shrugged. "I guess."

Travis had gotten my English Lit homework, so we worked on that. That didn't take long, so Travis and I decided to watch a movie. He got up to go pick something out and while he scanned through the movies, his phone, which was right next to where I was sitting, started to ring. He asked me to look at the caller ID and see who it was.

The caller ID didn't display a name, so I just told him the number that came up.

"Um… Doesn't sound familiar…just ignore it…"

I clicked the red button to ignore the call, and then something crossed my mind. I never thought of it before, probably because Travis' calls to me always displayed his name.

"Travis, you got a Texas area code on your cell, right?"

"Yeah," he said as he still looked through his movies.

When Adrianne and Tyler left, I was told that we would not be able to contact one another. I wasn't even sure if those orders came from Loren or Anne, and I just never even tried to call them, mostly because I didn't want to put them in unnecessary danger, even though I would have given anything just to hear Tyler's voice… They probably had to change their numbers anyways, but there was a chance they hadn't, and if someone else called in and from another area code… Neither Loren nor Anne would ever know about the call.

"I need a favor," I said to Travis

He saw me holding his phone.

"Sure… What is up? Wanna prank call someone?" He laughed.

"I need you to call a friend of mine, and well…and my boyfriend."

Travis looked at me, puzzled. I asked him to call Tyler first.

"You are going to tell me what is going on, right?" He asked, curious.

"Yeah…later though." I just needed to come up with an explanation that would not put Travis in danger, after all, there was no telling that his tattoo, the one with the protection symbol would really do what it was supposed to.

He dialed Tyler's number.

"Disconnected," he said.

I figured it would be, but I was still disappointed.

"Still want me to try the other one?" Travis asked.

"Nah. It is probably disconnected too."

He noticed my disappointment. "You can't be sure until you try it… That is the number for your boyfriend's sister, right?"

I nodded.

"Yeah, I definitely want to hear this story." Travis said. "Give me the number…you said her name is Adrianne, right?"

"Yeah."

Travis dialed Adrianne's number.

"Umm, hi... Who is this?" He asked.

"Loren?" He asked repeating the name.

I quickly motioned for him to hang up.

"Sorry, Loren. I have the wrong number." Travis quickly hung up.

I came up with another idea. One of those ideas that really gets your mind going... I thought about Adrianne's job in the vampire community, if you could call it that. She was sort of a vamp therapist, and helped newborn vampires with their transition. I figured that I could probably use that to get her on the phone.

I was so excited with this idea that I kept on talking and poor Travis could barely keep up.

"Okay, plan B. Call him back, apologize for thinking you had the wrong number and ask for Adrianne. I'm sure he will ask who you are. Do not give your last name!" Travis had the same last name as Loren, and I tried to convince myself that was just some creepy coincidence. "If he asks what it is about, say it is about work and that Adrianne's boss.... What was her name...? Right! Madeline. Say that she asked you to call and that you have instructions that she needs to be alone before anything is discussed...and when she is, just give me the phone."

Travis looked confused, but he was also laughing. "Jeez girl!!! Slow down. Write some of that down, there is no way I will remember all that."

I stopped Travis right before he hit redial.

"If you get her on the phone, remember that she needs to be alone before I can talk to her…and make sure you don't say my name." Ugh, this is so not gonna work.

Travis still had that confused look on his face.

"What? Are you afraid someone with bionic hearing will recognize your voice or overhear me saying your name?"

I sighed. "Never mind. This is not going to work."

Travis kept me from taking his phone and quickly hit redial.

I could hear Loren's voice from the other side of the call.

"Hello."

Travis turned the volume up, so that I could hear. He didn't seem to be as nervous as I was. "Oh, hi. I'm sorry, I just assumed that I had the wrong number before, but is this where I can reach Adrianne?"

"Who is asking?" I could hear Loren's cold tone.

"This is Travis. I'm calling on behalf of Madeline."

"Madeline who?"

Crap! I didn't know Adrianne's boss' last name. I started to panic.

Luckily, Travis was good under pressure. He sounded confident and very convincing.

Travis imitated Loren's cold tone. "It is work related."

Loren didn't say anything.

My heart started to race even more than it already was.

The phone line went silent and we weren't even sure if he had hung up and then, within a minute or so, Adrianne picked up the phone.

I felt so much better after hearing her voice.

"Who is this?" She asked, sounding suspicious.

"This is Travis—" I scribbled on a piece of paper for him to mention my last name…somehow… just a little clue on what this was really about. And I really hoped that Loren wouldn't pick up on that in case he was still around, listening in.

"I need to speak to you about Montgomery. Madeline said to make sure you were alone when we spoke about that."

I gave him thumbs up.

"Montgomery? ... Oh! Yeah. Is Montgomery with you?"

I was relieved that she caught the hint.

"Yes," Travis confirmed.

That was when I noticed there was something off about Adrianne's voice. I could hear the tension, the concern. "And is everything okay?"

Travis sounded lost in the conversation. "I guess so, I'm really not sure."

"Look, I'm going to have to call you back. It shouldn't take long. Can I reach you on this same number?"

Travis looked at me, expecting a response. I nodded.

"Yeah, no problem," he told Adrianne.

I just hoped that she would be able to call back before it started to get dark, before I had to go back home.

Chapter 25

Adrianne didn't take long to call back, but still, those were the longest minutes of my life.

While we waited for her call, Travis kept asking me what was going on, and even though I couldn't tell him the truth, I didn't want to lie to him either. I couldn't even focus on what to tell him, so I just said that I would tell him later. Noticing how anxious I was about the call, he eventually agreed to wait until later for me to tell him what was happening.

My anxiety must have been contagious because when the phone rang, Travis jumped up and answered it right after the first ring.

He put the phone on speaker.

"Hello."

Adrianne sounded concerned. "Okay, I'm alone now. Who are you?"

I grabbed the phone and took it off speaker.

"Adrianne, this is Lexi."

She sounded a little more relaxed now. "Oh, good. I hoped you were involved with the call. Please tell me that Tyler is with you… and who was that guy who called?"

I felt like my heart skipped a beat. "What do you mean?! Tyler is not here. Is he on the way? I called for him but…"

She cut me off.

"Alexis, who is that with you?"

"Travis, he is a friend from school."

I glanced at Travis and he seemed to be minding his own

business, he was now playing a game on his computer, but I knew that he was likely listening to every word that I was saying, which meant that I had to watch everything I said.

"Human?" Adrianne asked.

"Yes. What is going on, Adrianne?"

"Does he know about us?"

"No." I was now afraid something happened to Tyler, my concern showed in my voice. "Is Tyler coming? When should he be here?"

Adrianne was silent for a while, but it seemed like forever.

"Adrianne?"

"Lexi, Tyler left days ago. He felt as if something was wrong with you. He said that even though he was following orders, it was a mistake to leave you there alone in the first place. He said that he was going back for you and that he would never leave you again, even if he had to turn you for that to happen. I couldn't even believe he was considering that."

I started to panic. "Have you tried calling him? His number is disconnected, but I'm sure he has a new one."

"Yes, I tried, no one ever answers. I left several messages and nothing…"

"Can't Loren call him, you know call him!" I stressed the word calling, so that Travis wouldn't think I was crazy. I was doing my best not to make Travis suspicious about what was really going on.

"Loren thinks Tyler is working on a case with me. Tyler asked for help to get away from Loren's vigilance, so I helped him and now we are all screwed… I'm just going to have to tell Loren… But we will find him, Lexi. Don't worry." She tried to sound convincing, but that was not enough.

"How can I not?"

"Lexi, just don't do anything stupid. I need you not to call on him. If he is trapped by someone, he will be compelled to get away and depending on what kind of situation he is in, that could make everything worse."

Hearing that made me feel even worse. Only a few hours ago, that was exactly what I was doing, calling on him.

I realized Adrianne sounded suspicious of where he was or who had him.

"Where do you think he is, Adrianne?"

"Lexi, we will take care of it. And I need you to stay away from Anne until we get there. I was able to find a few things on that journal that I took from your house, which may be related to her. If my assumptions are correct, she is a different kind of immortal. She is more powerful and I'm not even sure there is a way to destroy her."

"So, you think that Tyler is with her?"

"I'm not sure, Lexi. Just keep your distance. Things that hurt us may not hurt her."

I was getting irritated. I was not going to wait for them to get here, it was too late for me to help Matt, and I was not going to wait to help Tyler. I couldn't risk losing him too.

"But Adrianne, whatever she is, she is half vampire so I don't see how the same things wouldn't hurt her."

Everything got quiet… Including Travis' computer game that was now paused.

Crap!

Travis had turned his chair around, and he was staring at me, eyes wide open in disbelief.

I couldn't believe I just blurted that out!

Travis didn't say anything, he didn't move. He just sat there, listening to the rest of the conversation.... just waiting for me to be off the phone.

Adrianne instantly realized what I had done. "Um, Lexi, unless we can find Tyler soon enough to take care of the boys memory...well, we just can't take the risk..."

She didn't have to be specific about what would happen to Travis.

"You can't touch him!" I blurted out.

I messed up and now I had to protect Travis. I didn't even care that he was still listening; it was too late for that anyways. He already heard too much.

I avoided looking at Travis. I couldn't face his reaction, not yet.

"Adrianne, that protection symbol on my necklace, he has it tattooed on him." She started to say something but I cut her off. "... and his last name is Crowel."

I had no clue what must have been going through Travis' mind. I took one quick look at him and he just sat there, with his head down.

I couldn't begin to describe how tense Adrianne sounded. "I guess we will figure out what is going on when we get there. Until then, the boy is your responsibility, Lexi. Tell him what you feel you should, but do not leave out the consequences of him knowing what he does… Loren will not be pleased about any of what is happening, but he won't leave Tyler without help. Honestly, I don't even think that Loren will leave you without help, which is odd considering his relationship, or lack thereof with humans."

"How soon will you get to Tyler?"

"Well, depending on the flight, we won't be there until sometime tomorrow and then we need to find out if Anne really has him."

Not soon enough.

"Do not do anything stupid, Lexi." Adrianne said in a warning tone.

I hung up. I looked at Travis and said, "We need to talk."

Chapter 26

I knew that telling Travis what was going on would be difficult. I didn't know where to start. Hell, I didn't know what to say at all.... I was completely speechless.

Travis met my gaze. "You were not kidding, were you?"

I shook my head. It was too late to lie about it, Travis was the type of person who would be poking around until he found out the truth, and it was better if I was the source of that truth.

I expected Travis to be flipping out by now, but he actually looked and sounded calm.

"So, your roommates... are they?"

I nodded.

"And this other Crowel family?"

Another nod.

"You think they are related to me, don't you?"

"Yes, I do." By now I realized that the star tattooed on his back was in no way a coincidence. It had to be Loren trying to protect his descendents.

"Holy cow!" He blurted out.

Okay, not the expected reaction. He was surprised, but he wasn't worried, or scared, or even thinking that the world as he knew it was turning upside down. He just seemed fascinated by it all.

"Travis, you can't tell anyone. And my roommates, they can't know that you know."

"What, you think I'm crazy enough to go around saying that?"

I attempted a smile. I remembered that had been my first reaction when I found out what Tyler was…. that if I told anyone, they would have thought I was crazy.

I was honestly surprised on how well Travis was accepting the truth.

He looked at me as if we were having a normal day-to-day conversation.

"Why didn't you tell me before, I mean, if you thought I was related to them?"

"Trust me, you would have been better off not knowing."

I caught Travis staring at a movie poster on the wall… Dracula.

"You know, they are not exactly like that…"

He grinned. "Kinda figured, being that the bloodsuckers are walking around in freaking day light!"

"Not all of them can do that though."

He looked at me, curious to hear more, and just like that I told him what I knew and about how the Crowel's were different. It was way more information than I should have volunteered, but the more I told him, the more relieved I felt not to be the only human I knew carrying this burden around.

He listened to everything I said, not once interrupting me. When I was done he smiled and said, "That is kinda cool, you know, possibly having a relative around from hundreds of years ago…. The drinking blood part is not so cool though… Gross!" He made a gagging sound.

He actually made me laugh. I was confident that out of everyone I knew Travis would be the one to keep this a secret.

"So, will this tattoo really protect me? He asked.

"In theory," I said in a warning tone, clearly insinuating that he better not try testing it.

I showed him my necklace, the one with the locket, which had the same exact symbol as his tattoo.

"Huh, who would have thought that this family tattoo tradition actually had a true meaning."

I heard a noise coming from downstairs…loud enough to make me jump.

Travis laughed. "It is just my dad, he is usually home from work around this time…he is not the quietest person in the house."

I had lost track of time. The sun was already starting to set.

"I need to get home."

"Lexi, there is no freaking way that I'm taking you back to that house! I'm sure mom and dad will let you stay here… Heck, they will probably insist you stay in my room!" Travis was really laughing now. And he was probably right, and it was funny in a way.

I insisted that I would be fine, and explained that Matt could still be out there, and that in a way, I would actually be protected at the house.

"Wow, you are just a vamp magnet, aren't you?"

I grinned. "I guess."

"Won't the necklace protect you from Matt?"

I looked down, avoiding his gaze… Hurt by the memories that flashed through my mind. "Necklaces can be removed."

“I guess we need to get you to a tattoo shop.”

“Yeah… That is so not gonna happen!”

After much arguing, he finally took me home, making me promise to call him if I needed anything.

Chapter 27

I was glad to see Travis drive off and go back to the safety of his home. I didn't want him around that night. Not for what I was about to do.

I knew how cliché it was to go looking for trouble, but I couldn't take the chance of losing Tyler, and if Adrianne believed that Anne had something to do with him being missing, it was likely that was exactly what had happened.

I had to find out what Anne's problem with me was. If I was able to find out what she wanted I could just give it to her, put an end to her little games and get Tyler back. Worst case scenario, if she didn't have Tyler, I could just give her what she wanted and leave without putting my parents at risk, and go look for him.

I couldn't go directly to her and I knew that my best options would be to find out what she wanted from either Nicholas, or Lars. Only, Nicholas was too smart, he would never cross Anne... and neither would Lars, at least not willingly, but I had to get information through one of them.

I decided to go looking for Nicholas; I knew that I was unlikely to succeed but at least I could trust him. He might have refused to give me information, but he wouldn't go running to Anne and tell her about it.

I was just about to walk out of my room when I glanced at the mirror and the image of Lars trying to drink my blood rushed through my mind. That was when I knew exactly what I needed to do.

I went downstairs to find Nicholas glued to his video game, Lars reading a book, and there were no signs of Anne being around.

I knew that for my plan to work, I would need to be alone with Lars. Fortunately, I knew that Nicholas was so focused on that game that it would just be a matter of waiting for the right time.

At first, I thought about giving Lars a note to meet me outside, but he probably wouldn't do it, besides, when I glanced at him, I noticed that he was almost done with the book.

I went to the kitchen, which was right next to the room where we kept the bookshelves, along with movies, and another TV, and I waited for Lars to come in that direction. While I waited, I opened the fridge and grabbed one of the bottles that they kept in the back of the fridge and put it inside the front pocket of my Gap hoodie.

When I heard the office door open, I went in after him, locking the door behind me.

Lars was scanning through the books. He didn't even turn around.

"What do you want?" He asked in a cold tone.

I took a deep breath and sounding more confident than I expected I said, "I want to know what Anne wants from me."

Lars turned around, met my gaze, and laughed.

"And you think that I'm going to tell you?"

I shook my head, not looking away from him, not showing any weakness. "No, I don't expect you to just tell me, and that is why I have an offer for you… You can have some of my blood in exchange for your answer. No one will ever know."

He grinned. "If you are talking about that bottle of blood that you have hidden in your pocket, you can forget about it."

I already expected him to say that, but I kept playing along. Making him believe that I wasn't actually willing to allow him to drink from me would make my offer even more desirable.

I sighed. "Fine! You can drink from me…but no biting."

"Huh! You want to know what she wants… here is your answer; she wants revenge."

Annoyed and even more confused, I asked. "Revenge for what?!"

Lars enjoyed seeing my reaction a little too much. "The deal was one question, sweetheart. You wanted to know what she wants and I told you… What are you willing to offer for more answers?"

Just the sound of his voice started to make me sick.

"Not a damn thing."

I turned around, unlocked the door and started to open it.

Lars' tone changed from pleased and sarcastic to angry. "Hey! The deal was that I get to drink your blood. Lock the door!"

I turned around just enough to where I could meet his gaze, and this time, I couldn't help but to smile. I can play this game just as well as he can.

"True, but I never said when you get to drink it, so I'm thinking…um…several decades from now, sucker!"

I quickly opened the door and walked out of there as fast as I could.

I went straight into the living room and sat by Nicholas, where I knew that I was protected.

Lars was so angry when he walked into the living room that he ignored Nicholas when asked what was going on, and left.

Nicholas went back to his game, while I sat there thinking about how things couldn't get any worse. I had Anne, coming after me, apparently because of some kinda of revenge that I had no clue what it was about; Tyler was missing; Matt was probably back to suffering the effects of his bloodlust and maybe trying to find a way to get to me; and now, I just added one pissed-off vampire to that list.

I sat there for what seemed like a long time, just staring at the TV. After a while, Nicholas turned the game off and went upstairs. I stayed on the couch watching TV, until I eventually fell asleep.

* * *

It must have been around two in the morning when I woke up after hearing a loud noise coming from outside.

I got up, still not fully awake and looked out of the window.

Travis' car was sitting outside.

My initial instinct was to open the door and go see what he was doing, but instead, I got my phone to call his cell.

As I grabbed the phone, I saw that I had a text message.

"Hey Lexi. Couldn't sleep... Don't like you staying at that house. If you are up, text me back."

"I'm up. Come on in."

Still looking out of the window, I saw Travis open his car door and walk towards the front door.

It only took me a few seconds to get from the window to the front door, yet, a lot must have happened.

I opened the front door and froze in place when I saw Adrianne rushing Travis back into his car, as someone who seemed to be Loren, fighting off two guys who I had never seen before.

I knew that Travis would be fine as long as he was with Adrianne; yet, I stood there, debating whether I should run to his car or go back in and lock the door.

I didn't even get a chance to make my decision.

I felt something hitting the back of my neck. I didn't pass out or anything, but the hit was enough to make me dizzy and disoriented. Within seconds, whoever that was, had my hands tied on my back, and something covering my eyes.

I screamed, but no one came to my rescue. Whatever was happening outside, Loren and Adrianne were probably trying to protect Travis, and I was glad about that.

After a few minutes, everything was quiet. I gave up on screaming, or trying to get away. And then, I felt icy cold hands picking me up. In silence, I was carried to a car and driven away.

Chapter 28

I didn't know where I was being taken; even after the blindfold was removed, I still had no clue. All I knew was that the guy sitting in the back seat with me was a vampire, and he wasn't the one who took me from the house, he just smelled different, like he had bathed in really cheap cologne. He was tall, strong and looked older than most vampires I had met so far. The way he looked at me was also creeping me out.

After being ignored when I asked questions about where I was being taken, I ended up spending most of the drive just staring out of the window. I knew that screaming wouldn't do any good because, well there was a vampire sitting next to me and it was clear that he was not a nice one. I thought about grabbing my cell phone and calling Nicholas, but the vampire had taken that as well.

After a while, he handed me the blindfold, well, he threw it in my direction. My hands were no longer tied and he ordered me to put the blindfold on. Not like I had a choice… I did as he ordered me to.

Finally, the car stopped. I was freaking out, but I tried my best not to show it. A warning, don't show weakness, kept popping in my head. Wherever he was guiding me to, it felt cold, and I thought I could hear and feel rats running by.

Don't scream… don't scream. I kept telling myself.

When he took the blindfold off, it took me only a few seconds to adjust to my surroundings. It was a dark room, probably a basement. It was surrounded by brick walls, lit up by nothing but candles. Across from me stood a woman who made me feel cold and nervous. I recognized her right away… Scarlett. And then I saw Matt standing just a few steps behind her. His stare was blank and it was almost as if he was under some type of spell. Anne had been right, it was only a matter of time before he was once again infected by the bloodlust that was destroying every hint of humanity within him.

Scarlett's minion, the one who had brought me in, held me back.

"Welcome to my home," Scarlett said, with a cynic smile.

That had been one of her hideouts.

I didn't even have time to ask what she wanted or who was behind all of this.

I heard a weak voice calling out my name just from behind me, and my heart stopped for a few seconds.

Scarlett's minion gave me enough room so that I could turn around, and there was Tyler, sitting on a chair with silver chains wrapped around his wrists and ankles, holding him down and physically hurting him.

Don't show weakness. Overtaken by anger, I was able to stop the tears from coming and I turned to meet Scarlett's gaze.

"What do you want?" My voice came out with more confidence than I actually felt.

Scarlett's voice sounded sweet and friendly, not quite matching her expression. "I just want to have a little fun. We have a common friend who thought it was a good idea to bring you to me. Said you needed a little assistance in making a choice and thought that I was just the right person to help," she smiled again, and then continued. "So, choose now. Matthew or Tyler; one may go free and the other will stay at my mercy."

I met Matt's gaze once again, his eyes still cold, with a blank stare. The Matt from before the accident had vanished. I then looked back and met Tyler's gaze and I could feel his pain. The imprint was still there; it was just hidden in my subconscious. I could feel how much he loved me and I knew I loved him just the same.

For a split second I almost just begged her to let Tyler go, but seeing Matt by her side, I couldn't allow myself to give up on Matt. I kept wondering if the real Matt was still there somewhere. I now knew that my blood could possibly save him again and I knew that if he stayed, he would not have a chance to being that Matt ever again.

Scarlett started to look annoyed, and impatient. "Child, the fun part of my evening only starts after you make your choice, so choose or I will make that choice for you."

I looked into her eye, my gaze locked on hers, "I choose me. Let them both go, please. I will stay in their places."

"No!" Tyler hissed. He sounded a little stronger and when I looked at him I could see the desperation in his eyes, but I had no other choice.

"Well, this is an interesting turn of events." She looked as if she was deep in thought. "Anne will not be happy about this at all… hmm…"

Tyler spoke once again, but this time I could not make myself meet his gaze. "Lexi, don't do this, please. I will stay."

"Hush!" Scarlett ordered Tyler. "That is an interesting offer, child, but I will make you an even better deal. For now, I will allow all of you to go, I can't really keep you until Anne is done with her little games … Her stupid little revenge is more about Loren than you anyways. I don't suppose she plans on turning or even feeding on you, which means that I can have you afterwards."

This had been the second time I heard about this so-called revenge. I interrupted her babbling. "What do you mean about this revenge with Loren?"

Scarlett's smile was even wider. "And the fun begins, already! I figured by now at least Tyler would have figured out what is happening."

I glanced at Tyler, and he seemed to not have a clue about what she meant.

Scarlett continued. "You know, at first, I thought Anne was just obsessed, thinking that you, Alexis, is the reincarnation of someone named Lydia, the one she holds responsible for her becoming what she is today."

Tyler listened carefully.

For a moment, I thought I heard him say something, but it was unclear. His voice was weak, and it made me want to go running towards him, but I was still being held back. I had a feeling that if I tried to get away, Tyler would have struggled to break free from those silver chains and he would get hurt even more.

Tyler managed to raise his voice. "What does that have to do with Loren?" He asked.

Scarlett wasted no time in continuing her story. "Well, so it seems, Lydia was Loren's lover. There was a lot of history between the three of them, and as I said, I believed Anne was just going insane with this obsession, until I heard of Loren's attempts to keep you away from Alexis."

"That can't be true," Tyler mumbled.

I wasn't even able to process everything that was being said. All I cared about was Tyler, and he just looked hurt, physically and emotionally and all I could do was try and comfort him from a distance.

"Tyler is right. That can't be true. If it was, I'm sure I would have felt a connection with Loren, and there is nothing." I meant every word I said.

"You may be right, child. Either way, none of that concerns me… As I said, I will allow all of you to leave."

I knew it wouldn't be this easy to walk out. "What do you want in return?"

"You are very smart. Before you leave you must agree to my deal…well, let's call it a contract, binding by blood. Once Anne is done with you, you will be my property, body and soul."

"I beg you, Lexi, don't do this, please," Tyler said.

Scarlett faced her minion. "Alexander, allow Matthew to go back to his accommodations."

He nodded. "What about the other one?"

"Tyler should stay…Just send someone else in to keep an eye on him." Then she faced me. "So, do we have a deal?"

Before I could respond I saw that someone was walking in through the door where Alexander and Matt had just left. I felt relief to see that it was Nicholas. I wasn't sure if he was older or stronger than Scarlett, but I hoped he would be able to get us out of the situation we were in.

Nicholas walked in confidently, giving me his best smile and then he walked towards Scarlett, kissed her hand and said, "It has been a while Scarlett, but you look just as stunningly beautiful as ever."

She smiled back at him. "Welcome back, Nicholas. And thank you for bringing me the girl. Now, please keep an eye on the boy while Alexis and I finish our deal, will you?"

I felt a jolt of pain in my chest. Nicholas nodded at Scarlett, then looked at me and winked. "Sorry love, that whole humanity brotherly thing had to go. It was making me as weak and pathetic as your boy toys."

This was it. No hopes of getting out of it. Scarlett had somehow manipulated Nicholas, or maybe he had been faking his friendship all along. I was irate, but there was no going back.

Scarlett asked me once again. "Do we have a deal? Yes or no?"

I looked at Tyler and whispered, "I love you". There was a tear of blood running down his cheek and I was no longer concerned about not showing any weakness and I could feel my own tears.

"I love you too, Lexi. That is why I'm begging you, don't do this."

I looked down avoiding his gaze. "I'm sorry, I have to." I looked up at Scarlett and wiped my tears away. "We have a deal."

Chapter 1

My life had been pretty normal until that point. I went to a private high school in LA, where I lived with my adoptive parents. I did pretty decent at school, especially for someone who didn't try very hard. I had awesome friends, and an okay boyfriend, I mean, I thought he was great at the time, but a lot of people saw him as a jerk, but whatever… Boy! Was I wrong?

That day, I woke up, and then spent probably the next half hour scanning through my closet. On a normal day, we would wear the school's uniform, but the school principal gave us a free pass that day, since we had a field trip. As long as we were dressed in what he considered decent, which was code for boring, we didn't have to wear the school's uniform.

I went downstairs, grabbed something to eat and walked out the door, getting in my Audi R8, that I had just got for my birthday. It took me forever to talk Kelly and Andrew, my adoptive parents, into getting me that car. They had the illusion that I was gonna drive some kind of SUV!

Andrew and Kelly were great. They pulled me out of foster care when I was about to turn four years old, so they were like my real parents; the only parents I knew, but when it came to safety, they were a little over-protective.

So… school field trip! Who would have thought that would mess up my so-called normal life?

* * *

We weren't at that silly museum but for a couple of hours. And then, my boyfriend Justin pulls me aside from the class because he wanted to talk. Like he couldn't talk at any other time of the day, right?

So I followed him into one of the rooms along the hallway and just as soon as I got the hint that he was trying to break-up with me, I turned things around on him.

"Yeah, I wanted to talk to you too," I said.

And then I jumped right into what I wanted to say before he could break-up with me first.

"This isn't working out, Justin."

He seemed surprised at first and then he just looked totally pissed-off.

"Well, glad you agree, because I have been kinda dating your friend Ashley too."

Okay, minus one on my awesome friends list. Lucky me, I could put on an act; not showing any reaction, I looked into his eyes and said, "Good. You two are perfect together."

Justin turned around and stormed out of the door. What did he expect me to do? Cry and beg him to stay?

Needing a moment to get myself together, I closed my eyes and took a deep breath. I was good at putting on an act, but that didn't mean that wasn't hurtful. Okay, I had only been dating Justin for about a month, but Ashley had been my friend for a long time.

Point was… that tough act, was just that, an act. Yes, I was just 16, but I had already learned how to hurt people before they could hurt me. That was my own defense mechanism. I would break-up with boyfriends, (not that I had many until now, I mean, I was only 16) as soon as I thought they were about to break-up with me. I would end a friendship as soon as I saw a friend come closer to someone else. It just made things easier.

Ashley kinda caught me off-guard though. Ugh, I hated when that happened. I was furious and I really hoped that my two other friends, Jess and Emily didn't know about it.

Right away I knew I would have to get to them before Ashley did. Ashley could have Justin all to herself, but I wasn't gonna sit and watch her take my two best friends too.

Unfortunately, me knowing that I needed to find Emily and Jess as soon as possible, wasn't enough to make me rush out of there. I ended up hanging out in that room for a while. Not because I found anything interesting in that room, on the contrary, it was all a bunch of junk… but I used my time alone to check my text messages and totally lost track of time.

I took another deep breath and just when I was getting ready to walk out of that room and go try to find the rest of the class, I heard a noise from the room next to the one I was in. I was afraid that whoever that was, had heard Justin and me earlier, and would go on to spread rumors around the school. I instantly thought that rumors were the last thing I needed, although that was inevitable. Still, I couldn't help myself from going into that room to find out who that was and how much he or she had heard.

I walked in there and at first I didn't see anyone. I heard someone sobbing, but that was it. I took a look around and in the back of that room, behind this awful old looking desk there was a girl hiding.

"Umm, hey. Are you okay?"

The girl turned around and it was clear that she was looking scared. I assumed she was probably lost. She looked younger than me…. probably about twelve years old, and I felt sorry for the girl, because whoever shopped for her clothes was in deep need of a visit to the mall, or maybe some fashion magazines.

The girl didn't say anything.

"I'm Kayla. What is your name?"

"Carolyn," she said, still sobbing.

I was trying to rush; I really had to catch up with the rest of my class…

"Are you lost, Carolyn?" I asked.

She nodded.

I looked out in the hallway, and saw a tour guide.

I turned back around to face her and let her know someone who could help her was on the way, but the girl was gone.

"Okay then…"

The tour guide approached me.

"Need help finding something?" he asked.

I told him about the girl and he said he would take a look around. There had been a couple of other schools there that day. Then he used his walkie-talkie to find out where my class was.

So, I had missed the entire field trip. Not that I really cared…

Outside, everyone was already getting into the school bus. I saw Justin and Ashley, all over each other, but what I was pleased to see were Jess and Emily as far away from them as they could have possibly been, and they both looked disgusted.

I noticed that a couple of people stopped what they were doing when they saw me walking out of the museum. It was one of those moments when you feel as if everyone is watching your every move. They were probably trying to catch my reaction in seeing Justin and Ashley together, but I just lifted my head up, smiled, and walked towards Jess and Emily.

They both waited until I got there and then, Jess whispered, "What the…"

I quickly interrupted her. "I dumped him. He must had seen it coming because apparently he had been with Ashley for a few days, I guess…Oh well!"

"But…we didn't know you were thinking about breaking up with him," Emily said, sounding disappointed.

"Sorry guys, I kinda wasn't sure about it at first, I wanted to be sure it was definite before I told you."

Emily sounded more cheerful now. "That makes sense. Well, it looks like you made the right choice. I just can't believe that skank would go after him like that though."

"Eh… I guess they are kinda perfect for each other in a skanky kinda of way," I laughed.

Jess, Emily and me all got in the bus to go back to school to face a day that was about to get weirder and weirder.

Chapter 2

On the ride back to school, I talked my best friends' ears off. That was my way of showing them how much I didn't care about Justin and Ashley.

Justin and Ashley sat a few seats in front of us and every once in a while, especially when we laughed out loud, Justin tried to discreetly look back.

I guessed the way I turned things around, breaking up with him before he could do that to me, really got to him, because he didn't look too happy.

Jess and Emily were already spreading the news that I had been the one who broke-up with Justin, and it was obvious that once he heard that everyone knew what had happened, well, what I manipulated to happen, Justin would be even more furious.

We finally got to school and Jess, Emily and me walked towards the parking lot, when we heard Ashley calling out to us.

"Hey guys, wait! I need a ride."

I turned to Jess and Emily, "She must be kidding, right?"

They both looked back at Ashley and gave her an evil look that I was glad I wasn't on the receiving end. Ashley didn't say anything. She just turned around and went the other way. Jess and Emily said they were going shopping and asked me to go, but as much as I hated to say no, I had to catch up on my chores before Kelly started taking away my privileges.

Last month, I had actually hired a cleaning service to get my chores done. This month, those four hundred dollar boots put me in a hole for the month… but it was well worth it.

I got home, did my chores, which took way longer than I expected. Then, I did my dreadful homework while I watched some lame reality TV show. It was one of those that was so pathetic that you knew you were just never gonna get that time back, yet, I couldn't turn away from the drama.

Kelly and Andrew had car pooled that day, so they got back from work at the same time.

Andrew said that he was taking Kelly out to some charity event for his work and asked if I minded ordering some take-out, which was way fine by me.

After eating some yummy pizza that I would have to work out triple hard at the gym to get rid of all those calories, I grabbed Kelly's laptop (I wasn't allowed to have a computer in my room)… and went to my room.

My room was actually pretty awesome. I had no complaints there. It was huge and well furnished, other than missing a damn computer…

I walked in, turned the lights on, put the laptop on my bed, took my shoes off and got on the bed, getting ready check into Ashley's Facebook to see what kind of lies she was already making up.

My cell phone ringing scared me to death. I had actually changed my ring-tone that morning and I totally forgot about it. I looked at the caller ID to see that it was Justin.

Umm. I was kind of curious to know what he wanted… So I finally picked up the phone, probably right before it was about to go to voice mail.

"What?" I said as I answered.

"Kayla, don't hang up!"

"Fine! What do you want, Justin?"

"Kay, I made a mistake. I am sorry. We are the ones who are perfect together… Can't we just like, get back together?"

Okay, didn't see that coming. I was tempted to say yes, just to get back at Ashley. I could always break-up with him again in a day or so.

I was just about to agree when I heard the sound of someone sobbing coming from outside of my room.

"Kelly?" Sometimes, she didn't answer, just to get me to call her mom..."Mom?"

Nothing.

"Is everything ok, Kay? Is that a yes or no, to my question?" he asked before me even answering whether I was okay. Jerk!

"Justin, I don't have time for this, I gotta go," and I hung-up on him.

I walked to my door and the sobbing seemed more distant than before.

"Andrew? ... Anyone home?"

No answer. Great!

It sounded like the sobbing was coming from downstairs. I followed the noise, holding my phone and having it ready to dial 911, even though the smart thing would have been locking myself in my room and calling someone. I always made fun of scary movies because people never think things through, and make the dumbest choices...funny how that is just human nature, and acting on instinct is not always a good thing.

I got downstairs, walked into the kitchen and the door leading to the basement was opened.

"You have got to be kidding me!"

I went to the kitchen counter, grabbed a knife and continued to follow the sobbing sound, which was just…strange. It was almost as if that sound had a volume switch, going from extremely high to barely noticeable at times.

"You know, whoever you are, I already called the cops, so you might as well just show up now," I lied, hoping that would scare whoever that was.

I opened the door to the basement all the way, grabbed a flashlight and went down the stairs.

The closer I got, I realized how more familiar that sobbing sounded. Okay, so now I'm getting paranoid.

I used the flashlight to see inside the basement, but there was nothing…. just that sound. When I reached the bottom of the stairs, I turned the basement light on.

The noise was coming from the closet. I put my cell phone down, and firmly grabbed the knife with both hands to stop myself from shaking so much. I walked towards the closet door. Freeing one of my hands from holding the knife, I swung the door open as fast as I could.

I didn't know if I felt relieved or freaked out.

Sitting all curled up in the corner there was the lost girl from the museum… Carolyn.

Also by Daniele Lanzarotta.....

About the author:
DANIELE LANZAROTTA
is the author of the Imprinted Souls Series.

She enjoys reading and writing young adult novels with just about any sort of paranormal or supernatural bent ... vampires ... ghosts... Daniele currently lives in Virginia Beach, VA with her husband, daughter and two lovable puppies (who are not really quite puppies anymore), Stitch and Gizmo.

This book can be purchased through Daniele Lanzarotta's web site,
www.DanieleLanzarotta.com

Also, please become a Friend of Daniele's
at the following social site addresses....

www.facebook.com/DanieleLanzarotta
www.twitter.com/danilanzarotta

You may also purchase this book at
Rocket Science Productions' web site,
www.rsp-llc.com

If you would like a free consultation about publishing
your book or music, you can contact us at the following...

Rocket Science Productions, LLC
5765-F Burke Centre Parkway, #222
Burke, VA 22015
info@rsp-llc.com
703-764-8000
866-509-4242 (toll free)